BARROOM BRAWL

The gambler, crouched, met the charge white-cheeked, both fists blurring. They drove High Pockets back a pace but did not stop him—hardly checked him. A long clean left to the gambler's chin exploded like a paper bag. Frodsham went back on his haunches and before he could collect himself, a slamming right spread-eagled him on the ground.

Dusty, disheveled, Frodsham clawed erect with grunting curses. They were like two beasts, snarling, growling, striving for the kill. Body struck body. The sound of that meaty impact sent a shiver down Rosalee's spine. When she could look again, Frodsham had both arms wrapped around High Pockets' torso and Hague's blurred fists were drumming the gambler's ribs.

TRIGGER-FINGER LAW

Nelson Nye

LEISURE BOOKS 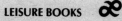 NEW YORK CITY

*Every character in this book
is entirely fictitious and
no reference whatever is intended to
any living person*

A LEISURE BOOK

Published by

Dorchester Publishing Co., Inc.
6 East 39th Street
New York, NY 10016

Copyright©MCMLXVII by Nelson Nye

Printed in the United States of America

TRIGGER-FINGER
LAW

1

THE PRONTO HOMBRE

For a long time no sound had come from the Parshall living room—but now sound came in plenty. Raucous, blasphemous sound; the noise of a man's loud cursing.

Rosalee Parshall, owner of the great Tailbone Rafter spread, had just sacked her foreman and he aimed for her to know he didn't like it. "By God!" he roared, "you can't pull that stuff with me! No damn' chit of a—"

"You've been misinformed, Ballard," came Miss Parshall's firm cool voice. "I not only can, but *am*. No Frodsham—"

"Frodsham! What the hell's *he* got to do with it? You listen to me, girl—"

"Suppose you listen to me for the moment, Ballard. I can overlook a good many shortcomings if a man is on the square—if he's faithful to his salt. I say I can put up with a powerful lot. But when I discover a low-down sneaking Judas ready to sell—"

"By God, that's far enough! 'F you're meanin' *me*," flared Ballard's growl, "you've got the facts backwards! I guess," he said, real quiet and ominous, "that goddamn bronc-stomper's been throwin' his jaw around some more!"

Over by the bunkhouse, some thirty yards removed, three lounging punchers exchanged significant glances. "Seems like, Clay, that fella's discussin' you," remarked the black-hatted rider to the young gent in the scarlet shirt.

Clay Roberts scowled. Unloading his jowls of down-tobacco, he hitched up his chaps with a sigh. "Expect I'm goin' to have to bat him down," he observed, and heaving himself from the bench, started tight-lipped for the house.

The third of the trio eyed the black-hatted hombre and grinned. "Stan' by to pick up the pieces, boy!"

A fourth man, a little apart from the others—a stranger leaning against his rat-tailed roan while waiting to see the boss—left off his cigarette building to stare after young Roberts curiously.

Observing the moment, the other two gave him a covert stare.

He was long, a tall sandy-haired man—big enough to hunt bears with a switch. Shoved back from his hard-bitten face was a steeple-crowned hat with flaring brim worn cuffed to a piratical slant. His batwing chaps were obviously new, but the rest of his outfit looked mighty like something a cat had clawed out of the ragbag. His shirt was so faded and patched, its original color would have to be guessed at, but the big Chihuahua spurs he had hooked to his boots flashed like the jewels of Opar.

He packed no hardware but a belly gun and wore that parked by his navel.

His name was Hague and he'd been christened Peter by fond parents in the hope he'd emulate that Apostle and tread a godlike path. But it had been a long time since anyone had called him Pete —nowadays they dubbed him "High Pockets" because he was so tall he could stop his bronc by dragging his feet on the ground.

Feeling the punchers' covert scrutiny, the stranger swung his head and ran a morose eye across them. His lip corners quirked a bit at the alacrity with which they found other things to occupy their attention. He was used to nosy hombres and had a way with them—a fact he was plenty ready to demonstrate on any and all occasions.

He'd learned a lot during the years he'd been upon this mortal soil; quite enough to convince him that the ways of peace and rectitude were the best ways after all. This was why he'd trekked from turbulent Texas to mingle with the red-shirted Cousin Jacks of Silver City; it was there he'd heard about this famous Tailbone Rafter. One of the greatest ranches in New Mexico, it had miles and miles under wire and ran twenty thousand head of graded cattle. It was an empire in itself—the envy of all its neighbors—and its sole owner was a lanky red-headed girl who had scarce turned twenty-one.

High Pockets shook his head. The women got the breaks all right—it was the very first law of nature. And what they couldn't get through luck and plain inheritance, they had a quick slick way of wangling from weak-minded has-beens over-burdened with this world's goods. Oh, yes! Never talk to him about women! He'd learned his lesson thoroughly; knew them inside out!

It was at this point in Hague's cogitations that Clay Roberts strode into the ranch house. The slamming of the screen door roused Hague and he finished his smoke, put it in his mouth and touched a match to it. Inhaling long, grateful drags of the pleasant smoke, he leaned against his rat-tailed nag and hummed an old range ditty.

> "While you are all so frisky
> I will sing you-all a song.
> I will take a horn of whisky
> For to help the sing along.
> It is all about a top screw
> When he is busted flat—"

And right there was where Clay Roberts re-appeared. Mr. Roberts was not walking. He came out with force and took the screen door with him and wound up tangled in a cholla. Folks must have heard his yowl halfway to Silver.

By the bunkhouse, the fellow in the black hat clucked solicitously. "Great Scott, boy! What'd you find in there—a Kansas twister?"

Young Roberts picked himself out of the thorns with a mean look in his eyes. He didn't stop to cut out any slivers, but grabbed his pistol and was heading ominously back, when Hague touched him lightly on the shoulder.

"Just a minute, son."

The bronc peeler's twisted look would have withered a budding yucca. But Hague was unperturbed; and something he must have read in the stranger's cold blue eyes appeared to check the angry snarl that hovered on young Roberts' lips. While he stood there undecided, Hague stepped up on the porch.

"I don't give a riprap if you own the whole blame state!" came Ballard's shouted curse. "You can't boot me out like some low pelado Mex! I—"

"You what?"

The soft drawl came from the doorway and Ballard spun with a blazing oath. He had a big and rocklike figure and a cold-jawed face that was wickedly creased in a scowl. A beefy face gone taut and dark with rage.

His narrowing glance met High Pockets' lounging posture and change broke the set of his features. "Who the hell are you?"

"The name," High Pockets drawled, "is Hague."

"Oh, it is, is it?" The foreman's scowl bit deeper; blackened. "This is a private wrangle, fella. I'll tend to you later. Have the goodness to step outside."

"Hmmm. Some guys does," Hague murmured thoughtfully, "an' some guys doesn't."

"Doesn't what?"

"Have enough pills in the think-box to get 'em in out of the rain."

The girl gasped sharply. Ballard's face was puzzled. Then suddenly the implication hit him. He came lunging forward with a curse.

High Pockets shrugged from his slouch and put five hard knuckles against the foreman's jaw as he went past. Ballard's head was like cement, but he staggered just the same, and when he turned there was a new look in his eye.

11

It didn't improve his tactics, though.

Probably been used, Hague thought, to slapping down anything that got in his way. He came boring in without a word and slammed a hearty right to High Pockets' face.

It missed because at the last moment High Pockets ducked. But the board wall back of the stranger cracked and splintered with a snarl. Then Hague bounced up from his crouch with a six-shooter in his fist. It took the foreman beneath the chin and Ballard went down for the count.

"You was sayin', ma'am—" grinned High Pockets.

The girl stared at him oddly.

But if she was fascinated, Hague was spellbound.

She was the best-looking piece of calico he had ever lamped in his life. She was a tall and willowy creature with long slim legs and a golden skin. She had a face cut like a cameo, framed by chestnut curls aglow like burnished copper where the sunlight brushed across them. And beneath her chin a golden throat curved softly to the open collar of her man's gray flannel shirt.

Looking up, he found her flushing under his scrutiny, and he blushed a little, too.

Then she said with a laugh: "You certainly showed *him* where to head in at!"

"Shucks," he said, "that wasn't nothin', ma'am. Got any more horn toads round you're feelin' a needin' to dispose of? Sidewinders is a species best stepped on when, where, an' quick as found."

"You stepped on him quick enough," she smiled, then frowned.

"Don't get me wrong," Hague told her hastily. "I'm a man of peace first, last an' always. It's just I can't noways abide to see that stripe of polecat annoyin' a woman."

Brightening, she gave him a smile that lifted his pulse, and it was plain she was considering something.

"Were you looking for work? You know cows, I suppose?" And at his nod she said abruptly: "Could you handle a job as range boss—I mean, *would* you?"

"Here?" asked High Pockets, startled. And when she nodded he gulped.

Foreman of the great Tailbone Rafter! It was any guy's chance of a lifetime and, without pausing to think, he said: "Sure!"

He knew a lot about women, but it looked like he had forgot all the things he had learned. And before he had chance to recall them, Ballard came to with a groan.

"Get up on your feet you big polecat!" Hague snapped. "Get up an' make amends to the lady."

Ballard got up all right—he got up with an oath and with curses spilling from his lips went wild-eyed for Hauge. "No slab-sided saddle tramp can pull that stuff with *me!*" he yelled, and slammed a hand at his holster.

He even got the hand curled around his gun grip—but as he lifted the pistol from leather all the rage drained out of his features and he stopped with a soul-shaking jolt.

13

Hague was twirling a gun by its trigger guard in the manner made famous by Curly Bill Graham the time he dropped the marshal at Tombstone.

"The road agent's spin!" muttered Ballard, and his eyes jumped out like two bugs on a stick. He reached for the sky in a daze.

Hague gave him a cold hard look. "Apologize an' git!"

The words jogged Ballard from hs trance. "By God," he said, "mebbe you ain't hep to it, mister, but you're pilin' up grief—"

"I've heard the wind hoot before," Hague scoffed. "You leave all that worry to me. An' clear out before I part your hair with a bullet."

Ballard's eyes stared back unblinking and he made no move to go. "I can get my way in this country—I got connections," he said slowly. "It'll pay you to keep on my good side. If it's work you're wantin'—"

"I'm up to my knees in work now. Save your breath to blow on your beans," High Pockets advised. "I'm not a patient man," he hinted. "Spill your regrets an' git."

He flipped up his gun in the Border Shift and Ballard started grimly for the door.

"Half a sec there, buddy—I ain't heard no apology yet."

Ballard flung round with a glower. "I'm sorry," he mumbled and clapped on his hat.

But High Pockets was not quite satisfied. "Round this patch of cactus that might be O.K., but where I hail from it's the custom to do the thing more elaborate. Tell the lady you been squallin' like a sore-backed bull; that you'd oughta had more manners an' will try an' keep a

14

civil tongue in your head hereafter. Tell her that you plumb regret your actions from the bottom of your heart an' are mighty sorry if you caused her any inconvenience. Say you're plenty regretful to be leavin' so swell a spread an' fine a boss, but that you know you had it comin' an' don't hold no hard feelin's. *Say it!*"

And with a curse Ballard finally said it, putting the best face that he could upon the matter. But the look he fixed on Hague when he had finished would have split a white-oak post.

Hague seemed not alarmed, though. He just grinned and said: "Lemme tell you somethin', amigo. I got the name of bein' a pronto hombre—quick to anger an' quick on the draw-an'-shoot. Keep junin' round an' you'll see."

2

A BRUSH WITH FRODSHAM

Where the mountains of New Mexico twist into the continental divide, the aspect in many ways is pretty terrible. The landscape there presented is severely rugged—majestic. A land of mighty crags and valleys, grotesque deserts, granite bastions, snowcapped peaks and dusty basins. Across its sagebrush wastes the winds have howled with fearful fury, yet its skies are brilliantly blue and its sunlight clear as the brushstroke of a master craftsman.

It was clear like this on the morning after High Pockets' hiring, and his heart beat a little faster as he knocked on the ranch house door.

"Come in," Rosalee's voice came briskly, and she looked up with a smile when he paused beside her, hat in hand. "There's a little chore you can do for me," she told him. "It's not a thing that's regularly a part of a top screw's duties."

She paused to regard him thoughtfully, a tiny frown putting momentary lines between her eyes. "The trouble is," she said, "there's nobody else around that I can rely on to tend to this

16

matter properly. My brother spent last night in town—I want you to go in and fetch him."

"Shucks, Miss Rosalee," Hague said smiling. "I'll have him out here in a jiffy. What's he look like? How's he dressed?"

"He looks a lot like me," she said; "you'll have no trouble on that score. I'm afraid, however, he'll not see fit to come. He's a good boy at heart," she went on hurriedly. "But he's a little rash—impulsive; he's hardly eighteen yet and he's got in with a pretty bad crowd. It's all that Frodsham's doing!" she confided a little fiercely. "He can wrap poor Tommy around his little finger—in fact, he's got him so I can't do anything with him."

"I see," Hague nodded, frowning. "He may not want to come. That's the idea, isn't it?"

She nodded. "I'm afraid it is. Frodsham has been trying to persuade me to sell him a part of this property; naturally, I've refused his offers. It isn't so much the price—it's just that I don't wish to part with an acre. Dad spent his life building this place up and I'd like to keep it just the way he left it. Frodsham's been encouraging Tommy to gamble . . ."

"Been trying to get a lever under you, has he?" Hague said grimly. "I think I get the picture, ma'am. What kind of a fella is this Frodsham—I mean, what's his angle? What's he do? How does he make his living?"

"He seems to have quite a number of irons in the fire," Rosalee told him. "He owns a couple fair-sized ranches. Then, over south of Silver, he has a manganese mine that brings him quite a bit of revenue. But mostly, I think, Frodsham's a

17

gambler. He runs the largest saloon in town and gets the lion's share of every pay-check issued on this range."

Hague nodded thoughtfully. "Pretty slick customer."

"Very slick," she agreed, and looked at High Pockets a little dubiously.

But if the new foreman noticed he gave no sign. "Whereabouts am I most likely to find this Frodsham outfit?"

"At the Red Onion, a saloon and gambling house on Bullard Street. It's below the bridge."

"You mean the Main Street bridge?"

She nodded, and he took leave of her, getting his rope and heading for the corral. He hoped there'd be no unpleasantness getting Tommy to come back.

Silver City was a copper town crouched restively in the south-flung shadow of the high Black Range—a place of unkempt hair and gusty oaths, of open-topped holsters and itchy trigger-fingers. A place where it paid a man to stay very much awake, as High Pockets knew. Placer mining had years ago removed about all the silver from the region, but there was plenty of copper of worth-while grade, and iron and manganese were scattered through its hills, as well as more than a trace of lead. A stone's throw away, at Santa Rita, was the world's largest open-pit copper mine, an affair first opened by Spaniards in the seventeenth century and still going strong under the guidance of red-shirted Cousin Jacks who, every payday, squandered largess upon the sporting gentry who ran the dives at Silver.

An old town but plenty lively yet, as Hague had reason to know, and he kept his eyes peeled as his rat-tailed roan picked its choicy way through the hock-deep dust of Bullard Street. New buildings were going up all around, frame, brick and adobe, replacing the older ones being leveled by the merchants moving from Main Street. There was little doubt, Hague thought, but that Bullard Street would soon be the liveliest part of town.

He found the Red Onion without difficulty and racked his roan among a brief line of other horses tethered at the hitching-rail. Close by was one— a fine bay gelding—whose hide bore the familiar mark of the Tailbone Rafter, and it did not take any crystal gazer to divine that it was Tommy's. Hague swung down and pushed his way through the swinging doors.

It was a bit early yet for the resort's day patronage to be present in any force. There were, however, several men—mostly miners and merchants—lounging in casual conversation along the bar. And over yonder among the tables was another knot of men; these appeared to be surrounding a table where a poker session was in progress.

There was no trouble at all recognizing Tommy. He *did* look a lot like Rosalee. He had the same sensitive lips, the nervous nostrils, the same shade of gold-brown eyes. But whereas Rosalee's chin displayed more than the average share of will-power and determination, Hague thought this lad's showed as great a lack of those sterling qualities. The lips were petulant, wayward, and where Rosalee's eyes were direct and challenging, Tommy's were reticent, guileful and inclined to roam if a man looked at him too steadily as Hague was looking at him now.

There was a good-sized pot in the table's center; three players, including young Parshall, appeared to have an interest in it. The fourth, a little swart-faced foreigner with bony shoulders and a scar across one cheekbone, was slouching back in his chair with thumbs hooked in the armholes of his vest, apparently well out of a losing hand.

Parshall was glowering at a long-fingered man in a black frock coat, who, with a quick glance at the remaining stack of chips in front of Tommy, had just pushed an equal number into the pot. "Reckon I'll just raise that twenty-five."

Tommy made no comment, but as he shoved the last of his chips to the center there was a sullen, badgered look to the twist of his eye.

The last player, a tall spare individual with high-boned cheeks and the air of a Southern gentleman, looked at the black-frocked man and smiled. "It's throwing your money away, Tranch," he observed, "and to show I'm right I'll up the thing another fifty."

"I'm callin'," Tranch said, and everybody looked at Tommy.

Young Parshall's face was a bitter study. His chips were gone and he held four queens in his hand. Hague said: "Tryin' to freeze the young gent out, boys?"

In the sudden quiet a host of eyes focused High Pockets in astonished scrutiny. Tranch's red and blowsy face came up in quick enquiry, and there was a chilled-steel quality in the considering appraisal of the Southern gentleman's eyes.

Without comment, both he and Tranch returned their stare to Rosalee's brother.

Tommy said with thickened voice: "How about another advance against my name, Clay?" and Clayton Frodsham, the man whose poised manner was so reminiscent of the Southern gentry, nodded casually.

"That's all right, Tommy—how much you want?"

"He doesn't want anything," Hague said grimly. "He's goin' home."

Through a room gone utterly silent, Frodsham stared at him. "Did you say something?" he asked finally, very softly.

"I said," repeated Hague, "he's goin' home."

Frodsham, running the tip of a thoughtful tongue across his thin lips, said, "I see," and after a moment asked: "Are you by any chance Mister Parshall's keeper?"

"Mister Parshall doesn't need any keeper. Being a sensible man, he can see he's being trimmed. He's decided to go home."

Frodsham's was the kind of face some people might have termed "horsey"—but there was nothing the least equine about the calculating alertness of his half-closed chilled-steel eyes. He said with a cool, tight smile, "Suppose you let Mister Parshall speak for himself."

Tommy, looking from one to the other of them, dark-cheeked, cried petulantly: "What the hell is this, anyway?" and with a surly glance at Hague, said: "I don't know you, sir, and—"

"You're going to, though," Hague murmured. "I'm the new Tailbone Rafter range boss. Better tell these tinhorns you've had enough."

A dull flash spread across the florid face of Tranch, and the bony-shouldered foreigner shot a glance at Frodsham in a way that asked for orders while he eased the thumbs from the armholes of his vest.

But Frodsham didn't look at him. He had put his cards down and was bleakly regarding High Pockets with the flats of both hands whitely pressed against the table. He said softly, very blunt with his words: "If you care to keep on bossing Tailbone Rafter, friend, I'd advise you not to meddle in things that don't concern you. Only for the fact that you're strange here and may not understand our ways, I'd have something to say to you about these choice remarks—"

"Them remarks," Hague said, "go just as they lay."

For the space of three slow heartbeats no one spoke or made a motion. Then Tommy, scowling, growled: "I'll thank you, sir, to tend to your cows an' keep your face out of my business. I'm old enough to know what I'm doing an' I can do it without any help from others. I'm—where's Ballard?" he demanded with sudden suspicion.

"Better ask Frodsham," High Pockets murmured. "Ballard's gone hunting greener pastures —he yanked his pin out yesterday, as you'd have known if you'd been home where you belonged instead of wasting your sister's money with these saddle-blanket gamblers."

"So I'm a saddle-blanket gambler, am I?" Frodsham inquired, leaning forward. "Have a care—"

The rest was lost in High Pockets' laugh. He

said, with his eyes on Frodsham, "If the scar-faced gent with the bony shoulders don't get them paws above the table quick, he's goin' to be found so full of lead you'll have to ship his remnants to a smelter."

A tight, packed stillness fell across the room. But Scar-Face had to be shown; he put frantic speed in the lifting hand.

Flame burst whitely from the region of Hague's thigh. The gun was smashed from the lifter's fist as it cleared the table. It was a shot no man but Hague would ever have dared attempt, and he grinned at the shocked expressions of incredulity that broke across the watchers' faces. It must have seemed to them like a miracle, for Hague's hands were as empty now as before.

But the gray, scared look of the scar-faced man was proof in plenty of the stranger's grim ability. Then the watchers caught their breath and a sneer twisted Tranch's red features. "Very pretty," he said sarcastically. "Ver-ry pretty indeed. What I'd like to know is how long you spent practicin' that trick?"

But Hague was all through fooling. He shot his left arm out and yanked young Parshall from his chair, shoved him roughly toward the door. "Get goin' kid. Get out there an' onto your bronc."

"You gon' to let this bird tell you what to do?" Tranch sneered.

One long quick stride took Hague to the gambler's side. "You triflin' gnat," he snapped. "Another crack out of you an' I'll knock you flatter than a last year's leaf!"

"Yeah?" said Tranch, and came from his chair with a curse.

23

"Yeah!" Hague said, and a mule's-hoof right packed up from his boot-straps sent the frock-coated man sprawling headlong. Hague didn't wait for the fellow to pick himself out of the tangle of chairs, but whammed his body round and put a raking glance across Frodsham's watching countenance. Lantern-jawed and lean-carved, the gambler's high roan face showed one brief flicker of fierce vitality; then caution was clawing its way across those wind-whipped cheeks and the man's narrowing lids had shut off his thoughts completely.

"Well!" High Pockets sneered. "Ain't *you* wantin' some?"

You had to admire the cool control displayed by the man's schooled features. The blue serge snugged the gaunter angles of his frame where he stood with hands hooked to pockets, looking Hague over calmly. Inscrutability lay among the ordered planes of that highboned face, and if his smile seemed a trifle Mephistophelean, it still was well in character, for there was an atmosphere about the man, an assured and cool conviction that he could rise to any emergency—that he could take any hand that was dealt him, stand pat and call for a showdown. There was, too, a grim hint of stealth, of stealth and guile and secrets dark—of things a man would best leave unexplored—behind the forbidding bleakness of his stare. This cool and poised erectness of the man brought to mind old tales of Morgan, of Spanish silver, Dutch doubloons—the creak of the oft-trod plank.

But Hague, brushing these impressions aside, thumped a balled fist upon the table harshly.

24

With a scorn that must have stung the man, he said again: "Ain't *you* wantin' some?"

Frodsham met his gaze unblinkingly. "No, friend," he said very softly, "I guess I can wait for mine." And somehow High Pockets, following Tommy out, had an uneasy feeling that this was no vain boast.

3

RIDERS BY NIGHT

Though High Pockets did his best to draw the youngster out, to find some topic of conversation that might interest him and be some kind of bond between them, the return to the ranch was made —on Tommy's part—in sullen silence. He rode with his glance fixed straight ahead, and something in the set of his shoulders promised an accounting when one could be managed to his liking.

The new Tailbone Rafter foreman covertly studied him. The lad was not much like his father, of whom Hague had heard a-plenty since his advent to this country. All the oldd man's better qualities appeared to have been left, with the ranch, to Rosalee. Perhaps young Tommy's crippled left hand had kind of warped his nature; it was knotted, shrunken, a stiffened stub, permitting only the slightest flexure of its under-sized, bony fingers. An accident of birth, Hague guessed, and felt a little sorry for him. Just the same, he thought, there were traits in Tommy not too well excused by the fact of a mere bum paw.

From a brassy sky the sun poured heat across the yucca-dotted miles. Now that the higher altitudes of the Pinas Altos Range lay back of them they were sweating at the mercy of a furnace draft flung up from off the desert. Black Mountain lay off there to the south and across its rugged eastern flank there showed the blue and wind-swept crest of distant Avalanche Peak.

They crawled across the lowlands with the sun dripping heat like melted copper and with the wastelands' eternal silence hemming them with a monstrous hugh like beings in a world apart; and so came at last in sight of the ranch with evening's purple shadows unrolling across the valley floor.

A smell of coffee and frying steak were in the air as Hague got out of his saddle, standing for a moment to watch a dusty Tommy yank the gear from his tired bay, slap the animal into the pole enclosure, flop his saddle across the kak-pole and go striding off toward the cook shack, silent still.

With a shrug Hague looked to the comfort of his own mount and, when he entered the mess shack minutes later, found the hands at table, chaffing one another as they gulped their steaming food. Talk took a lull when High Pockets entered, dropping into a chair at the table's head. Many of these men, he guessed, resented a stranger's being appointed over them; some were probably friends of the discharged Ballard and would keep eyes skinned for a chance of causing friction. It was Tommy, though, who had Hague worried.

By the time High Pockets had finished, most of the boys had rolled their smokes and drifted outside. When he came out he saw a trio of them with their heads together over by the bunkhouse; Tommy was sauntering toward the house, moving away from their direction. Hague looked after him with a frown.

There was something up—no doubt about it. Trouble feel was in the air and, with a smothered curse, High Pockets started for the bunkhouse.

The men broke up before he got there, and with a great show of casualness prepared to meander off someplace when High Pockets, recognizing one of them, called briskly: "Half a second, Smith. I want to talk to you."

The man addressed hung undecided for a moment, then muttered something in a lowered tone and his companions moved off several yards to wait for him.

"Now," Hague said, coming up to Smith, "what's all this muttering about?"

"Can't a man mutter if he feels like it?"

"Not on any spread I'm bossin'," High Pockets said without compromise. "If you got any kick, come to me like a man an' say so."

Smith, a chunky hombre, black-haired and with piercing black eyes set beneath thick brows that were like a tangle of catclaw, passed a horny hand down over his drooping mustache and let the lips beneath it curl. He was known as "Organ" Smith because he hailed from the Organ Mountains and was forever dragging them into his conversations. But he was not dragging them in just now.

"Like a man, eh?" he said, and looked Hague over insolently. "You mean like a *he*-man, Mister Hague, or like one of them squirts that comes from Texas?"

Hague had come from Texas and guessed that the others knew it. He eyed the man for a little, reticently, turning something over in his mind. Then when Smith hitched up his chaps and spat, he knew the insult had been deliberate and smashed a quick, hard fist against the puncher's jaw.

Smith's head snapped back and his body in a sprawling fall went snapping backward after it. But he was up with an oath and with the failing light glinting off the barrel of a pistol.

Hague hurled himself aside as the gun went off and, before the man could fire again, buried five hard knuckles to the wrist in the fellow's stomach. Smith went down, doubled up and gasping. Hague kicked the pistol out of the way and stepped across to the fellow's two companions.

"Feel like takin' it up where Organ quit?"

They didn't seem to like his looks. They backed away from him, carefully, keeping hands well away from their gun belts.

"What were you birds gassin' about before I came up just now?" he said, waving back the rest of the crew who were starting toward them curiously.

"We weren't gassin' about nothin'," muttered one of the pair, still backing. "Just arguin' the merits of Bill Jones' strawberry r—"

Hague's quick laugh was hard and short. "Always talk about horseflesh like you're speakin' of the mother lode?"

In the fading light the men looked startled.

Like caught fence-crawlers, High Pockets thought, and stared at them grimly. He was about to say something when someone, stopping beside him, laid a hand upon his arm. "What was that shot?"

Hague turned to face his owner. Rosalee's look was troubled. He said with an offhand chuckle, "Smith was cleaning his gun an' it went off— dang lucky it didn't kill him. Nothin' to get excited about, ma'am."

She looked at him a little curiously, but finally shrugged and turned away. She said over her shoulder, "Soon as you're free I'd like to see you up at the house."

He nodded and returned his gaze to the sullen-faced pair before him.

"Duncan," he said, "I didn't expect to find a guy like you mixed up in this underhand kind of business. I thought you were a man who could be relied on."

Gene Duncan looked away across the range, not meeting his gaze. He was not, Hague thought, a real top hand, but he was so close to being one that you couldn't get a hair between. He was kind of disappointed in a way, because he'd rather cottoned to the dark-eyed, black-hatted puncher. It rather looked as though his confidence had been misplaced.

"What about you," he said, addressing the other man. "You feel like loosening up?"

But like Duncan the man kept his mouth shut.

"All right," Hague said. "If I find further cause to watch you birds, I'm makin' out your time."

Wheeling, he went back to Smith who was up now and hunting for his gun. "I'll see you over at the office, Smith. Step over there soon as you find it."

In the office he dug up the time sheets, figured out how much Smith had coming and wrote a check. When the man came in he pushed the green slip toward him. "Pack your bag and hit the trail."

Smith stood glowering for a moment. Then he grabbed up the check and started for the door. "One thing more," Hague said. "I'd advise you to get off this ranch and stay off. Next time you're going to get hurt."

Smith slammed the door behind him. Hague stayed at his desk for a number of thoughtful moments. He would have to keep an eye skinned out for that fellow. If Smith had done a little ranting, forcefully describing what he had in mind to do, High Pockets could have forgotten him inside five minutes. But he hadn't.

It was a most significant fact.

"What," asked Rosalee firmly, "was happening out there?"

"Why," said High Pockets twirling his hat, "I done told you about that, ma'am. Organ Smith was cleanin' his gun an—"

"That why you discharged him?"

"Well—" Hague's cheeks showed a trace of color. "Er—"

"Stop stalling. I want the truth, Hague. Tommy told me you'd got rid of the man and wanted me to hire him back. Now I put you in here to boss the place, and I'm executing you to boss it. But I *do* think I'm entitled to know what's going on. Don't you?"

"Certainly, ma'am. No one got a better right."

She looked at him sharply. "Then suppose you

loosen up a little and tell me what it's all about."

"That would be a pretty tall order, ma'am. You see, I don't rightly know myself—"

"Don't know!" She looked at him suspiciously. "You know why you discharged that fellow, Smith, don't you?"

"Well, yeah, I guess I do, ma'am—"

"Stop ma'aming me! Look here; are you going to answer my questions or aren't you?"

"Since you put it that way, ma'am," Hague told her slowly, "I reckon the answer's 'no.' "

"What?"

"I said I reckon I'm not goin' to."

There was a brief, an intense pause. The girl looked distinctly puzzled. She was regarding him as though he were some strange critter from out of another age. She said at last: "You refuse to answer my questions?"

High Pockets nodded. "I'm afraid I do, ma'am." There was a brief twinkle far back in his eyes as he met her angry gaze. "Every place I ever worked on, the top screw had the say as to who was hired an' fired. He did his work without let or hindrance from the owner. If you ain't satisfied with the way I'm doin', why, I reckon it's your privilege, ma'am, to hunt up another range boss."

Her eyes had widened in amazement; her breast was heaving. She seemed unable to believe her ears. "Do I understand you to mean you'd like for me to do that—to get another range boss?" she asked, astounded.

"Well, no. I'm pretty well satisfied with this job, if it comes to that, ma'am. I'll tell you— it's like this: When I hire on to boss a place, I

32

expect to boss it. Not much sense to a fella roddin' a spread unless he's got the owner's confidence."

She seemed pretty much bewildered. High Pockets stood, hat in hand, regarding her gravely while he waited for her decision. She took a nervous turn about the room; came back to face him, frowning. "What I can't understand," she said, "is why all this mystery. You fire a man, I ask to know the reason and you give me this talk about a foreman's rights." She eyed him as though expecting some solution.

Hague nodded gravely, a faint smile curving the corners of his lips. "That's right, ma'am. You've stated the case exactly."

Exasperation put twin spots of color in her cheeks. She looked as though she'd like to shake him. "I believe you are the stubbornest specimen I've ever come across. What am I going to do with you?"

"The Lord only knows!" said High Pockets piously, and his face abruptly broke up into a lot of curves and angles. "Mebbe," he said, chuckling, "you'd better get rid of me, Miss Rosalee. You know," he said, rasping a hand across his chin, "how some fellas go round with a willow stick an' bring up water? Well, that's the way I am with trouble. Ol' Man Turbulence just seems to waller in my tracks."

She couldn't seem to make out whether he were joking or serious. But finally, with a sigh, she appeared to make her mind up. "Trouble," she said, "seems to be clustering round the rafter of its own accord. There were certainly plenty of clouds along the horizon before you came, and I guess another cloud or two won't make a whole lot of difference. I expect I'll keep you on awhile."

She smiled and Hague smiled with her. "Despite your infernal reticence," she said, "there's something about you that I like."

Back in the shanty placed at the disposal of the Tailbone Rafter foreman, High Pockets lit the lamp, sat down in a chair and put his feet upon the desk—only, however, after first taking the precaution of pulling down the shades. After all, he had no guarantee that Organ Smith wasn't lurking someplace handy with a rifle, waiting for a chance to safely even up accounts. Then there was Tommy, too, who held a grudge against him, though High Pockets did not think young Parshall would resort to such extremes. But he had literally lived with his life in his hands for several years and found habits like caution and vigilance not easily relaxed. There was another habit that clung to him stubbornly, also—the habit of suspicion. This eternal probing of others' acts, this seeking to find what lay behind them, was as natural as taking coffee with every meal. He had this need for detail and it kept his keen mind working.

It had it working now.

What connection, he was wondering, lay between such men as Ballard, Frodsham, Tommy and Organ Smith? So different each in outward seeming, some strong tie yet bound these men together—this much he knew for fact. Ballard and Smith obviously found their interests, for the moment anyway, identical with Frodsham's; they were, High Pockets believed, in Frodsham's pay.

But where did Rosalee's brother fit into this picture? What was the bond that caused young Tommy to string with Frodsham?

High Pockets could easily see how a youngster of Tommy's caliber would find something dashing, a strange macabre attraction, in the cool, dark poise of the gaunt-framed gambler. He could see how the lad might find reflected glory of a sort in basking in the limelight of so hard and public a character. But he could not find any reason for Tommy to be stringing bets with a man of Frodsham's caliber.

Hague could grant a certain amount of magnetism to the boss of Silver City; the fellow had definite charm when he wanted to display it. But it seemed to Hague that here was something more than youthful hero worship; after all, he'd made it plain to Tommy this morning that Frodsham and his friends were out to trim him. That should have antagonized Tommy—to at least have caused resentment. But all the resentment High Pockets had observed had been directed against himself.

He could not forget that Tommy had been talking to Smith and those two others and had found business elsewhere when he'd seen Hague coming up. Nor could he overlook the fact that Tommy had tried going over his head to get Smith hired back. These things added up to something if he could only find out what it was.

There was more to this than met the eye.

But figure as he could and did, High Pockets was forced at last to the conclusion that here was a nut he could not crack—at least, not yet.

He'd often found a ride of benefit to the solving

of knotty problems, and decided to take one now. There was nothing like good air to sweep the cobwebs from one's mind. Going to the corral he roped himself a mount—a big, black gelding with legs that were built for speed. His gear strapped on, High Pockets stepped into the saddle. Most of the boys, he observed, had gone inside; he could hear the muted mutter of their voices and guessed they had got themselves occupied with a game of stud-horse poker.

He took a trail leading north and east, toward where the frowning outline of the Black Range's rugged mountains shoved dark ramparts like a wall against the sky.

The night was black as the bottom of a well. Big stars shone out, seeming hardly a good rope's throw above him, but their light did little to illumine the vague terrain. The moon was not yet up and Hague gave the horse his head, letting him go where he had a mind to. Where they went made little difference to him; he could think as good one place as in another, just so there was the feel of a moving horse beneath him.

This night, however, High Pockets' thoughts were more than ordinarily restless. He had Rosalee Parshall in his mind and could not get her out. Never had he met a girl like her before; he found himself wondering if indeed there were any others like her. She seemed so definitely individual; so spirited, brave, and yet withal so sweet. He found her personality disturbing, upsetting the ordered pattern of his mind. In some odd way it made his pulses tingle just to think of her. How short a time he'd known her! Yet he could recall each curve and gesture, every contour of her features, and the exhilarating abruptness with which she spoke her thoughts. The time was coming, he thought a little wistfully, when she'd make some gent almighty happy.

The thought of Rosalee married somehow made the loneliness of this land more potent. It turned him moody and he quite forgot the business that had taken him on this ride.

The moon was getting up now and a rougher wind shouldered down from the timbered slopes. He rode with an increasing awareness of the gulf that lay between them, a separation made not alone by wealth—the inheritance that was Rosalee's, but made the greater by his own past mode of living.

A man who long had held emotion with an iron rein, he could not properly understand his feelings toward this girl who had come so abruptly into his life. That he was drawn to her he realized; the fact had to be faced. But the knowledge that there never could be anything between them had also to be faced, and it was this that scratched his temper, that was making him fight the charm of her. It was not the scars left across his memory by that Alamo Hashhouse biscuit-slinger; it was the knowledge that, the matter of worthiness aside, he had no business thinking that way of anyone. To push their acquaintance further, and he was by no means certain it could be so pushed, could mean but one grim outcome—sorrow and heartbreak for one or both.

The teeth of the matter lay back in Texas. He had left that turbulent land to put the past behind, to live his life as other men lived, in peace, security, without resort to gunplay. Yet here he was already embroiled in a fight he knew nothing about. It seemed that nowhere lay the thing he craved. With reputation sidetracked, he found himself entangled in other snares; new confusions and enmities reaching out of the blue to snatch at him. So he had ever found it in the past. Even here it was becoming so.

His father, a boomtown peace officer until checked mid-stride by a dry-gulch lead, had in his time made numerous enemies, a few of whom survived him. One of these, three-four years back, had found occasion to besmirch the old man's memory. With a gun in his hand, High Pockets had settled the matter; but the incident, like the cheese in the house that Jack built, had set his boots in a different path—a trail that had no turning.

By any measure it had been a lucky shot by which he'd downed Joe Branton. The fellow had been an irrigation crook, a man whose draw had shamed lightning by comparison. He'd shot first then, but Hague's had been the more accurate. And not yet had he lived it down.

Because of this he had resolved long since to live his life alone. There was no place in it for a woman—least of all a good woman. The dictates of his heart must be discounted lest they snare him into bringing grief to one who must in that event be dearer than life itself.

He had made this decision firmly, and lived up to it as well. But heretofore he had met no girl like Rosalee—he could not get her out of mind. Better far, it might be, he thought, were he to ride out of the country—right now, before it were too late.

He was debating this when a sound of hoofs, a dim far flutter wind-driven across the black opacity, roused in him the past years' care and vigilance. From where he sat the gelding this land sloped sharply to a yonder meadow across which the trail ran to climb the rock-ribbed gloom of hemming hills, cutting through them by a gap hardly wider than a wagon road.

Wheeling his head with muscles cocked he saw two horsemen briefly silhouetted against that space.

High Pockets knew at once what he must do. This was Tailbone Rafter range, even though it lay within the boundary of the newly-created Gila National Forest, and knowing the disposition he had made of Rafter's hands he could think of no good reason for a pair of riders being at this time in this vicinity.

He started cautiously forward, letting the wise horse pick its way. There was no reason for proceeding so carefully save the strangeness of the hour and place. But caution was an ingrained thing with him.

Coming off the meadow floor the canted trail led through the felted gloom of pines and all was a black-branched tangle through which the occasional shine of stars loomed briefly and was gone. Then the pines fell back and the trail rolled through the gap.

It was there that Hague dismounted; there that he had seen the men. He left the black on trailing reins and catfooted forward, crouched, and with a gun gripped ready in his hands.

4

BEHIND THE BRUSH

Dust smell, faint but unmistakable, came with
the gusty wind that was slamming through the
pass. From out the deep solitude of that curdled
black beyond, there rose a feel of wildness, un-
placeable, yet striking knifelike through him. His
shoulders swayed a little, restively. Then, stiffen-
ing, he crouched listening, while a turbulence
called up from other days, from other nights like
this, bent the corners of his lips, curving them to
that tight and white-lined bitterness that had
been known so well to the familiars of his past.
There was a knowledge in this wind that stirred
him, rocked him, calling for investigation. It
pulled him forward through the gap, crowding
one rocky wall with narrowed eyes that raked the
gloom.

The gelding nickered back of him and Hague
was thankful that the wind was blowing toward
him—away from those two riders who were
somewhere paused in the obscurity of that foglike
murk ahead.

He pushed forward, alive to the possibilities,

yet grimly determined to learn what had brought these men in dead of night to Rafter range. That the answer would be some way connected with the boss of Silver he had little doubt, and he went stealing forward slowly till he came to where his ears picked up the muted tones of a low-held conversation.

He could not see the speakers, but by the sound he guessed them to be somewhere back of the tangled brush that showed to the left in vague black lacings against the lesser darkness of the sky.

It was in his mind to rouse them out—to flush them into the open. But to use his gun would give away his whereabouts and, very probably, would be instantly followed by the scream of fright-slammed lead. He stooped and, bending low, reached out a feeling hand across the roughness of the earth to find some missile fitted to his needs. It closed about a stone and he rose quietly, listening; then, carefully gauging distance, drew back his arm and hurled the rock.

He heard it strike—a rustle sound absorbed abruptly in an utter quiet. The wind soughed eerily, whispering through the branches, and swiftly was gone—lost behind a crackle and snap of brush beat down by hurrying horses. They hit the hardpan of the trail and frantically the hoofs lashed out in a reckless gallop, urged on by lashing quirt and raking spur.

Hague did not fire. He waited grimly till the last faint clatter of their progress died away, then started forward, quartering through the brush till he struck their sign, back-trailing it to the site of that low-voiced conversation.

He struck a match. Cupped in his palms against the wind the flare showed half of a tiny clearing, boot marked and hoof marked. Then his raking glance swept in a thing that narrowed it, that brought again that hard twist to his mouth.

He snuffed the match and stood there, thinking, body braced against the shouldering of the wild. Frodsham was playing for big stakes—for bigger stakes than Hague had ever dreamed. No wonder he wanted to buy a portion of this property; even though the National Forest had closed down this section of the Rafter range, Frodsham wanted it. Hague knew now why the man didn't scruple to bring Tommy into his power as a means by which he might even yet force Rosalee to sell.

He nodded slowly to himself and pulled the wind-whipped foliage back across this thing his matchlight had disclosed. Once more he paused. Then, with eyes gone bleak and big fists clenched, he started for his horse.

5

THE BITTER SHADOW

There were no lights showing at Tailbone Rafter when Hague rode in, but a late moon hurling its yellow flood across the heavens made a pleasing picture, smoothing out harsh lines, making the most of its subject like the brush of a competent painter.

Hague unsaddled by the big corral, slapped his horse inside, and had just bent to lift his saddle to the kak-pole when there came a sudden *chunk!* and a gun's flat challenge ripped the night.

Half whirled around High Pockets fell against the bars, scraped down them to a sitting posture while a low, choked sob squeezed out between his teeth.

The night went very still. Even the insects seemed to have suspended their bickerings and there was no sound in all that space save from the occasional restive stamping of some horse in the big corral.

Seconds passed like dragging centuries. Then abruptly, with no more noise than the footfalls of a spider, a shape detached itself from the clustered shadows by the harness shed and with swift stealth stole closer to the moveless range boss. Twenty feet away it paused, body held crouched and rigid, while it swung its head from side to side like a dog when it keens the wind. Apparently reassured, the shape moved nearer while the moon struck reflections from a bit of metal gripped in a lifted hand.

Then out of the silence came a voice. "Careful, Duncan. I've got you covered." Malicious satisfaction edged the range boss' words.

They stopped the shape midstride. With a jar of breath it froze in its tracks.

"Drop the gun," Hague said. *"Drop it."*

With an evident reluctance the black-hatted man let loose of his weapon.

Hague stood upright. "Over to the shack an' get a lamp lit. Come on—mosey." He waited till the man moved off, then scooped up the gun and followed, keen eyes alert for trickery.

Inside the shack Hague slouched on a corner of the table regarding his prisoner grimly. Duncan's expression puzzled him. Defensive, sullen, resentful, it still was hardly the look to have been expected from a caught dry-gulcher.

"I'll hear your story," Hague said coldly.

"What's the use? You wouldn't believe me."

"Probably not. But you'll tell it anyway."

Duncan scowled. He opened his mouth a couple of times and shut it without committing himself.

"Come on," Hague said. "I haven't got all night. Start with the shot. Where were you when you heard it?"

Duncan seemed a little surprised. He said: "I was over by the harness shed—"

"*Why?*"

Duncan looked at him a moment. "Don't reckon that concerns you—"

"Anything that happens on this spread concerns me," Hague said grimly. "What were you doing by the harness shed?"

Defiance glinted from Duncan's half-closed eyes.

"All right," Hague said, "we'll come back to it. You heard the shot. Where'd it come from?"

"I couldn't make sure. If I'd been watching for it—"

"Make a guess."

"It seemed," Duncan said, "to have come from over by the house. I'd heard you ride in a little before that an' I looked to see where you had gone to, and—" He broke off, eyes intent, to listen. "Sounds like the boys pilin' out of the bunkhouse—"

"Never mind them. Get on with the story."

"Well," Duncan growled, "I couldn't make you out for a minute. Then I seen a dark shape huddled low against the bars. I says to myself, 'By grab, they got him!' an' started forward to see how bad you was hurt." He looked at Hague resentfully. "If I'd knowed you were playin' possum—"

"You're not Victor Hugo. Stick to your tale an' get on with it."

Anger edged Duncan's muttered words. "I'd almost reached you when I happened to think that bush-whacker might not of left. I took a squint around an'—"

"I know the rest," Hague cut in gruffly. "What about this empty in your pistol? What'd you shoot at?"

"If it had been *you,*" the puncher growled, "you wouldn't be here now."

They eyed each other across six feet of space. There was a sudden belligerence in Duncan's cheeks. "Lemme tell you somethin', bucko. You're not makin' yourself a heap popular around this place. If—"

Hague's smile, slow and thin, suggested mirth less than anything in the world. "I don't aspire to popularity," he said. "Which is fortunate, no doubt, because my talents"—here he tapped his gun—"are hardly the kind to grace a parlor." He stopped and let the silence gather. "You can go now," he said finally.

Duncan made no move. He faced Hague, hard, expressionless.

"What about my gun?"

Hague tossed the pistol at him. "Better watch your step."

It was still early when Hague knocked on the ranch house door the following morning.

"Come in," called Rosalee, and he entered the living room to find her watering potted plants. She looked clean and fresh and sweet in the morning sunlight, and the old hunger that he thought subdued rose up to plague him. There was a vibrant magnetism in her personality that drew him strongly, that put gaunt slants in his lean bronzed cheeks and hedged his tones with a harsh repression.

He stood against the wall, face grave, staring down at his dusty hat. He said: "I've found out somethin' that I reckon you ought to know.

There's copper on your northeast range. In place, not float—offhand I'd say it looks like the mother lode.''

He lifted his glance then, looking to find her startled. But she was not. A little astonished, perhaps, but nothing more. She set her tumbler down and looked at him composedly. "When did you find this out?"

"Last night."

She was startled now. She looked at him in quick inquiry, one hand spread before her breast, brown eyes gone dark and round. "Then it was you!" Relief came into her face and the red lips smiled at him suddenly. "Oh!—you don't know how you scared us! We thought it was some of Frodsham's crowd. . . ."

"Were *you* up there last night when I threw that rock?" asked High Pockets, more taken aback than he cared to have known.

"Is that what it was?" She laughed a little, recalling her fright. "Yes, I was there—"

"Who was that with you? Tommy?"

"No-o." She sighed. "Not Tommy—Gene Duncan was with me."

"Duncan, eh?" High Pockets said thoughtfully. "He's more active than a fly in a bottle now, ain't he?"

"Gene's all right," she said in quick defense. "I have the greatest confidence in Gene—"

"Been with you quite a spell, eh?"

"I grew up with him," she said. "His father used to own the Currycomb—one of Frodsham's outfits."

"How'd young Duncan happen to be with you las' night?" Hague eyed her morosely. "Ask him

47

to ride along?"

"It was the other way around," she said, and looked at him peculiarly. Her look was searching, appraising—just a little wondering. She did a strange thing then; she smiled. A strangely wistful, yet definitely pleased kind of smile. "He said he'd discovered something—that if I was game to take a little ride, he'd like to show it to me. We rode out to the northeast range—out to those homesteads Dad bought two-three years ago—the part of our range that's in the National Forest. That's the place you mean, isn't it? Just beyond the Gap?"

High Pockets nodded. He was doing some serious thinking, scanning what must lie ahead, trying to see a clear trail—trying to figure just how the cards would be most likely to fall. He said abruptly: "I expect you can see what this means, ma'am. This business is goin' to force Frodsham's crowd out into the open. Unless I miss it a mile, this business is goin' to mean trouble an' plenty of it."

"Wait—" She laid a hand on his arm and took a long deep breath while she eyed him searchingly. "This Gila National Forest is a new thing, you know; it's only been established recently and I don't know a great deal about it. But I understand all the country within its boundaries will be closed to entry—both minerals and homestead rights as well as grazing privileges being withdrawn; that cowmen and others having land inside will be forced to sell out for whatever the Government wants to give them. In which case, of course, we'll not be allowed to take an ounce of copper out of there.

"Wait!" she held up a hand as he would have interrupted. "In other words, any time now the Government is liable to be sending me a check and telling me to move on out. There doesn't seem much use in getting excited over this find— it's what I told Gene Duncan. What's the use in going ahead with anything like staking out claims and filing when the Government—"

"Half a sec," Hague said, and put his glance upon her grimly. "Who's been telling you all this stuff?"

"Why, let me see," she exclaimed, regarding him with something of puzzlement. "Most all the owners have been talking about it. Only the other day Ballard was saying—"

"Uh-huh! Ballard, eh?" said High Pockets scornfully. "I mighta known that polecat—"

Her regard was plainly astonished now. "Why —isn't it so? Won't the Forest people put us out?"

"Hell no!—excusin' my English," Hague said savagely. "I can see the hand of Frodsham back of this all right! Forest Reserves are put aside for use—for the use of the greatest number. The Government will lease the grazing rights, open certain sections for farming—"

"But I thought the idea was to conserve—"

"Sure—it is! The idea is to conserve, all right, but nowhere in the set-up are there any rules or regulations for ousting present owners. You say this Forest is a new one? Then the chances are they'll soon be opening agricultural sections to homesteading. An' as for mineral rights, anyone can go into a National Forest an' locate himself a mine. If—"

49

"You're sure of this?"

"Absolutely. If your father—or the men he bought 'em from—took out patents to those homesteads that make up your northeast range, nobody under God's heaven can put you out. They can't put you out, buy you out, or freeze you out. That land is absolutely yours!"

She looked at him, striving to comprehend this thing in its entirety. "Tell me some more," she said with a little laugh. "What are these Forests established for—just what is the idea back of them?"

"The idea back of 'em," Hague said, "is to insure a perpetual water and timber supply; to make it certain that the ranchers of this country will have an everlasting source of forage—to preserve wild game and such stuff. You can go any place in a National Forest an' camp or picnic, hunt an' fish. You can stay as long as you like—in certain parts, I reckon, you can even build yourself a home if you've a mind to. I've been in a couple of these National Forests an' I'm here to say they're a dang good thing! The Forest people want these reservations used—the greatest use for the largest number of people is their password. They'll probably establish some place in this region a 'wilderness' or 'primitive' area. The idea of this is to set aside some bit of country so that our grandchildren—people that have 'em, anyhow—an' *their* grandchildren, an' so on down the line, can come around an' see what this section of the country was like when the first pioneers came across it."

"I see," she murmured slowly. "Since this Forest land, as you say, is open to mining, the idea now is for us to stake that copper first—to get in ahead of Frodsham; to file location notices and rush copies in to town for quick recording. Isn't that what you've got in mind?''

High Pockets shook his head. "Didn't you say your Dad had taken patent to them homesteads?''

"To the homesteads comprising our northeast range? To that country round the Gap—the part that's been included in this newly-established National Forest? Yes—certainly,'' she said.

"Then that land is yours. Mineral rights are included in homestead patents. You don't *have* to file or stake—that land is yours right now; every inch of it, above and below the surface. As a matter of fact, it's yours more now than ever with this National Forest crowd behind you.''

She regarded him with a new, a deeper interest, as though surprised by his knowledge of these things. She put a hand on his arm again and was about to say something when his shoulders stirred impatiently and he backed off a step, shaking free of her touch. There was a ruffled look about him as he wheeled away and, taciturn, made a savage circuit of the room.

She watched him, wondering; a little hurt by his unaccountable brusqueness, a little breathless, an unexpected wistfulness briefly showing from her eyes.

But his back was turned; he didn't see. And change, when he wheeled again to face her, had driven all expression from her cheeks.

She said practically: "In a nutshell, then, this range is mine; lock, stock and barrel. With those patents protecting me in my mineral rights, as long as I hold onto them, Frodsham can do nothing. That's the long and short of the business, isn't it?"

Hague's morose glance passed round the room. He nodded. "Yes; that's the legal angle. Legally," he said slowly, "you can mine that ore or leave it where it is. As far as the law's concerned, you've got this ledge sewed up."

"Fine," she said with a smile. "Then we'll just let Frodsham whistle. That's good cow range and I've a mind to leave it that way; I don't think Dad would have cared to see it gophered full of holes. Rafter's got enough coin banked to get along on for a spell. When you pass the bunkhouse, Hague, you might tell Duncan to come over here for a—"

Hague said: "I'm not goin' past the bunkhouse. I'm not finished talking to you yet. *Legally* you've got the picture of this copper perfect. But there's another angle to this thing—it's the reason brought me over here so early."

Her brows went up. "You mean—?"

"There's such a thing as extra-legal methods, an' Frodsham ain't goin' to take this beatin' layin' down!"

"But you said," Rosalee exclaimed, "I had the ledge sewed up. That—"

"Legally, yes. But does Frodsham strike you as the kind of man to let such trifles stop him? Didn't you say yourself that he's been trying to *buy* that land? Yes. Well, you refused to sell, and by now he'll know you're wise to what he's after. Wait—" He held a hand up grimly. "Why do you suppose he's taken the trouble to plant spies in your outfit? You found out some way yourself that Ballard was taking Frodsham pay—it's my opinion Organ Smith was another of the same damn breed." He said nothing concerning his maturing suspicions of Tommy, but looked at her intently.

"Don't smile," he said. "This ain't no smilin' matter. Somebody took a shot at me last night when I rode in—whoever fired that shot has ridden straight to Frodsham with the news!"

Her cheeks had paled. She said incredulously: "You think someone trailed us up there—?"

"I'm sure of it. Organ Smith, I reckon. But—"

"Even so," she said. "Even supposing it *was* Smith, and supposing he's got to town and told them that we're wise—what can Frodsham *do?*"

"Do? I'll tell you," Hague said harshly. "It's what he *will* do, too! He"ll rush a bunch of hired men in there—gamblers, gun fighters, any riffraff he can get his hands on! He'll . . ."

"But you just said," she interrupted, "that I had the ledge sewed up with homestead patents. You said the land was mine, above and below the surface; that no one could touch it. That the law—"

"That's it exactly!" he broke in hotly. "The law! What law have you got in this country? One-man law, ain't it?—*sheriff law?* What do you suppose Frodsham cares about that? He probably owns your sheriff body and soul! The only kind of law a man like Frodsham ever heeds is the trigger-finger kind!"

She looked at him with set white cheeks. She seemed at last to have gathered something of his thought. In the refracted sunlight her eyes were

53

taking on a haggard, haunted look. She moved back a step, away from him, her glance hard on his face.

"You think in spite of everything they'll try a stampede on us?"

"I'm sure of it—it's Frodsham's only chance," he growled. "God knows I don't *want* to see it that way, but with this set-up it's the only answer." He eyed her grimly. "Don't forget for a single minute it was Frodsham discovered that copper! He'll not see that ore pass out of his hands without a fight; he'll stoop to any means he can think of that'll insure his getting it—that'll offer him even the *hope* of getting it!"

She nodded, almost imperceptibly; and High Pockets let the stillness settle while he studied the far-off look that shaded the brownness of the glance she put through yonder window. The forlornness of that gaze cut into him deeply, showing him how bitterly she fought this picture he was painting—how fiercely she must hate this forecast turbulence.

Well, he hated it, too. He'd come these many miles to avoid this kind of thing, to get clean on away from it. Yet now, as in the past, he still was faced by it;. he could not close his eyes to that which must lie ahead. The desire was strong in him to mount his horse and ride away—to get beyond some far horizon before the web of this new trouble should enmesh him as it had these others. There was no peace for him here. Unless he quit the country swiftly these quicksands looming so plainly in the trail would grab him, would force him into playing again that character he had sworn he'd put behind forever.

The old impatience tugged his shoulders, roused him. Rather late for sidestepping now; this thing had gone too far—he was a part of it, entangled by allegiance to this girl, entangled by those enmities he'd made already in this land.

He shrugged again. Why lie? He knew why he would stay. He would stay because of Rosalee— because of something she had roused in him that was stronger than himself.

He met her look. A trust showed there behind the other things; in this ill hour she turned to him for guidance, for help and aid and counsel. His regard was long and reticent, yet the hunger of him showed. For it was in his mind he'd never see her in this guise again. Events were shaped to patterns and this was an old, remembered one that did not change.

Experience had too well taught him the way of things. Reproach would drive this trust away from her. Reproach in turn would be crowded out, its small place taken by an awe—a fear of him and what he represented. She would see him soon for what he was: a grim and terrible machine for the smashing of raised barriers, for violence—destruction. It was his talent. . . . She would hate him before this thing was done.

6

"HOP AT IT!"

Her voice came softly now—intimate. "What must I do?"

"There's only one thing you *can* do, ma'am; you've got to beat him to the jump. You've got to get out there right off. In mining parlance that ledge will be called 'discovery'—it's on patented Rafter land. What you've got to do is stake out claims on the Forest land around it; there may be ore there, but it isn't likely. You've got to do this for your own protection—to keep Frodsham from crowding you."

A queer look worried the depths of her eyes. She said abruptly: "But won't that antagonize him more than ever? Won't he—?"

Hague said bleakly: "Yes. But we've got no way around that; we can't help it. He's bound to hit the warpath anyway. By now he'll have a good half of Silver on its way; he's going to play what cards he has to. The way those cards will fall is goin' to depend a lot on us—on what *we* do. Even if you sit back an' fold your hands, his play will be the same. He's a smooth-talkin' bird but he's goin' to fight, an' he's going to crowd the fight to you. Unless we got out there and stop him, you're going to see a boom camp planted on Rafter range overnight.''

He looked at her grimly. "Have you ever seen a boom town, ma'am? A hell-roaring copper camp?"

She shook her head. "I've been over to Santa Rita, of course, and out to Chloride Flats—"

"Those are old camps, ma'am. There's no comparison. I tell you plainly—a working camp is hell! But enough of this," he said, and squared his shoulders. "We'll stake those claims on Forest land; that'll keep the camp beyond them—it'll keep his riffraff from high-gradin' your bonanza. Have you got any location notices handy?"

She nodded. "There are some in the desk. The paper over at Silver prints—"

"You dig 'em up. I'll get some horses under saddle—"

"But if it's in Frodsham's mind to do what you're figuring he'll do, won't he have his men out there already?"

"No. It's forty miles to Silver. It was after midnight when that dry-gulcher took his shot at me. If he cleared out on the instant he could hardly have got hold of Frodsham quicker than five o'clock this morning. Don't forget, he was on a horse that already had made the trip to the Gap an' back. He'd be going some to reach Frodsham by five—even if he was lucky enough to find him soon's he got to Silver. It's only a little after seven right now. We've got time all right if we hurry.''

She said: "I hate to do this. It's going to mean

bloodshed, isn't it?"

He met that intent look she put upon him. He said harshly, "Yes. But would you let that fellow drive you off your range? Would you let him *steal* what you won't sell him? That's what it comes to, Rosalee. It's up to you. Make up your mind."

She stood a moment undecided, thinking. Squaring her chin, she nodded slowly. "Father always fought for what was his; he loved his Black Range country. He buried Mother here." She sighed. All the buoyancy seemed gone from her; all the light and all the laughter. "I'll fight," she said at last. "But it's terrible to think of—"

"Don't," he told her gruffly. "I'm your range boss. The responsibility is mine. For what may happen I'll take the blame." And he left her then, striding out into the sunlit yard.

Before the bunkhouse the lounging punchers eyed him curiously. They could not help but notice the change in him since yesterday. They could not know it, but they were looking at the man he had been now—the man he'd tried to leave behind. That cold, pinched look was about his nostrils, his wind-whipped cheeks were curbed to a tight, stiff slanting. It was a mask-like face they stared at—but one well known back in Texas.

He stopped several paces from them and beckoned the scarlet-shirted Roberts; called young Duncan, too.

He said without preliminary: "Duncan, I owe you an apology—I ask your pardon for what I said last night. My suspicions were unfounded."

Duncan nodded. There was a little flush upon his cheeks.

Hague turned to Roberts. "I'm naming you

wagon boss, Clay, with authority to run this spread under my orders till further notice."

Roberts stared. "You quittin'?"

"No. But I'm goin' to be a heap too busy to fool with ranch work. I want a man I can depend on here to keep the spread running smoothly."

The corners of his lips quirked slightly at the look on Roberts' face. He said then quietly: "I want five men who can handle rifles an' won't get cramps in their trigger fingers. I want 'em right away, an' I want seven broncs with speed an' bottom under saddle within five minutes. That's all—hop to it!"

He shoved him toward the staring crew, grabbed Duncan by the arm as the latter started after him. "Half a sec there, Duncan. You're in a bad spot. One of Frodsham's crowd knows you took Miss Rosalee out to the Gap last night. Unless you've a cravin' to be found in a gulch with your light blown out, you'd better keep your eyes skinned."

He left the puncher slack-jawed and strode away for his rifle.

7

A DEFINITE UNDERSTANDING

High Pockets had made it plain that his object was to get there ahead of Frodsham and they took the grade at a gallop. In Silver there were two of those newfangled gasoline buggies Mr. Ford was putting out; and while they were uncertain things at best, they could, when properly primed and pampered, make a bronc look like a snail. It was a leadpipe cinch that if the rush were not already under way, it would be mighty soon. As Hague had pointed out, this was no damn time for picking posies.

Once the news of this strike got out there would be a stampede started that would make hair curl! Every able-bodied man in miles would jump a horse to get here, and once the country was staked the riffraff would pile in like vultures.

It was not a time to waste in argument or in the fine perfection of plans; hard riding was what was called for and the horses were pushed to the limit.

By day this was a high and rolling country they were pushing into; the hills that rose like ranger hats off yonder across the dun terrain were pocked with rock outcroppings, brown and green and a-bristle with the sharp jade spikes of century plants, the prickly arms of cholla and the yucca's lancelike shafts.

Abruptly Hague thrust up a hand. "Let's slow a bit here, boys. No sense foundering these nags; we may be needin' 'em before we're done with this."

Accordingly, for the next half hour they rode at an easier gait. They were climbing steadily higher now, leaving the yucca-dotted range behind. Ahead lay a tumbled region of sharp-sloped desert mountains, rock and sand choked foothill canyons—a hushed and lonely country. Mahogany brush rose along the trail, and midway between their riding and the blues and mauves that marked the far horizon, bright red cliffs showed up like roosters' combs against orange crags.

They were entering the Black Range now and by nine o'clock they came in sight of the Gap. Hague reined in his bronc on the crest of a ridge. Swinging round in the saddle, he sent a raking glance to the south. He sat for long still moments and finally roused up with a grunt. His arm stretched out and pointed and there was no need for comment. Back there above Skillet Mesa a faint haze filmed the air. "All right, boys, let's go," he said, and put his horse through the Gap.

It was hot work beating through that brush, for the sun was well up now and even at this high altitude its rays burned like a glass. The men's eyes popped when they saw the ledge and several of them whistled excitedly. But Hague said nothing and his mouth was grim as he dug out the location notices Rosalee had given him and passed them round. "That fence down there the boundary?" he asked, pointing.

Rosalee nodded. "Yes."

"What you goin' to call this mine?"

She sat a moment with a tiny frown between her eyes. "You put a name to it," she suggested.

"Half a sec," Hague said, and brushed a hand across a jaw. Then he looked up and grunted. "We'll call it the Copper Girl—O.K.?"

There was a trace of pink in Rosalee's cheeks. "That suits me," she said.

"All right, boys," Hague looked them over. "Down beyond that fence now an' start staking your extensions. Cover all that slope an' don't leave any loopholes."

Hague sat his horse beside Rosalee, watching the crew clatter down the slope. She had signed all the notices at the house—Hague, too; filling in their names as witnesses. There was nothing for the men to do but pace off the claims and stack up stones for monuments. When they had finished Hague called them back.

"Here's the situation, boys," he told them quietly. "Miss Rosalee is satisfied with being the proprietor of Discovery; she's making you a present of them claims—"

A wild cheer from the hands cut him off. When the excitement had subsided somewhat, Hague said, "She'll give you boys all the time you need to prove up on them an' you'll continue getting your pay the same as if you were doing your regular work around the ranch. Half a sec, now—" he cried, holding up his hand. "This ain't goin' to be clear sailin'. You boys were picked because you know how to shoot. I'll not tell you what to do in the event anyone tries to jump your claims, but there's one thing I want to make clear: on no account are you to sell any of these claims to Frodsham—no matter what he offers.

"Now! Whose bronc is the least used up?"

After a moment "This dang bay coyote," said one man, slapping his mount, "has still got a heap of character."

The horse was a buckskin with dark stripes along its back. Hague's eyes were critical, but at last he nodded with a grunt of satisfaction. "All right, fella. What's your name?"

"Janes—Bill Janes."

"O.K., Janes. You're elected to ride to town an' file these copies with the county recorder. The law gives you ninety days to do it, but if you're wantin' to take a whirl at mining, I'd say the quicker these notices are filed, the better. Hell's apt to pop when Frodsham gets here. He knows about this ledge an' he's been tryin' to wangle Miss Rosalee out of it; tryin' to buy this range, lettin' on like he's intendin' to run cattle here." He looked Janes over sharply.

"Think we can trust you to go in an' get these copies filed?"

The man's cheeks showed a touch of color. "I reckon."

"All right. Get goin' then. Don't kill your horse, but get there, see the recorder an' come on back. We'll take care of your claim. But remember," Hague said grimly, "don't touch a drop till you've got those copies filed."

With a grin the man stepped into his saddle.

* * *

It was nearly eleven when the stampede hit the Gap. The ridge was hotter than Hell's backlog; even the greasewood and mesquite that tanged the lazy wind had a scorched smell to them and the snakes had holed up in the shade.

But heat meant nothing to that mob from Silver. Their minds were set on copper and their looks said they meant to get it. There was quite a howl when they saw the slope was staked below the Tailbone wire. But if they had reckoned without High Pockets, he had not done the same by them. Under his cold quick eye the men from Rafter stood pat on their claims—cold-jawed and with ready rifles.

On horseback and muleback, with sacks, picks and shovels, in spring wagons, buckboards and carry-alls came these seekers after copper. Bearded and shaved and whiskered they came— all kinds, creeds and colors. Ten-gallon Stet hats showed through the dust of their churning; flat-crowned, steeple-crowned, curly brim and stiff rim—there was even a sprinkling of derbies, and stovepipe hats bobbed through the haze like beavers at a political rally. There were red-shirted miners, hoemen and cowmen, be-jeaned and with Levi jackets, frock-coated gentry and gents with no coats on at all. Shirts plain, checked and striped vied colorfully with butchers' and bartenders' aprons. A motley crowd, with Frodsham well up in the lead.

He was in a high-seated horseless buggy with the blowsy-faced Tranch for a driver. Straight up to the Tailbone Rafter fence they drove and stopped with a series of snorts. Both men climbed out, ducked through the wire and hurried to where High Pockets sat his horse beside Rosalee.

Frodsham whipped off his hat with a flourish. "Guess you're Miss Parshall, ma'am?" he inquired, and when she nodded, his bow showed a drawing room smartness. He stood a moment then, staring round with a smile. "Goin' to be *some* camp," he declared with a chuckle. "Great days ahead, Miss Parshall, ma'am—great days. Is this," he asked, turning, "where the copper was found?"

Hague eyed him coldly. "There's the ledge right up there—you can see it all right where you are."

Frodsham looked. He wheeled his shoulders back round with a laugh. "Well," he said, "you made a lucky find, Miss Rosalee—a mighty lucky find, ma'am. Hope you've left a little for the rest of us fellows—"

"Right down there," Hague cut in, waving a negligent arm toward where his men stood with rifles. "Right down there, Mister Frodsham, sir. All forest land and free for the taking—beyond what's staked already, that is. Don't believe I'd monkey with that if I were you—those boys down there mightn't like it."

Frodsham took a look at the Rafter hands. His manner was politely casual; and when he brought his face around there was an amused kind of smile about the corners of his mouth. He said nothing for the moment; but his sleepy lids, rolling slowly up, showed how the glint of his eyes had changed. That glance, reaching past the watching Hague, came to rest on Rosalee.

"There's a deal of work hooked up with the development of a mine. Things often come up," he said reflectively, "which a woman would find un-pleasant—perhaps impossible to cope with." He spoke as one old friend advising another. "Naturally," he added smoothly, "I wouldn't be expecting such things to come up in *this* case. But a person can't always tell. No one, for instance, would think of buying apples, let us say, by the color of their skins. The wise man regards prospective mines in much the same manner. A nice-looking ledge is just a ledge until the shaft is sunk or the tunnel driven. One may find bonanza, or find that the color has pinched out. Mining, in my experience, is pretty much a gamble; a game in which, with the uninitiated, money is more often lost than gained.

"How many of those fellows," he asked with a negligent wave of the hand toward the staring townsmen lining the fence, "will have the fortune to locate copper here?—or to know it if they do? I don't wish to seem discouraging, ma'am, but mining is a chancy business at best. Now I've had considerable experience, an' I've been wondering, ma'am—" He paused to give her a searching look; "I've been wondering if, perhaps, you might not be anxious to annex the services of a practical partner?"

"Meanin' you?" demanded High Pockets before Rosalee could answer.

Frodsham brought up his regard from the hat still held in his hand.

"Why, yes," he said, his glance very cool and sharp. "I guess, if there were no one better qual-ified available, I'd be willing to act in that capacity. I might," he added reflectively, "even

66

consider advancing the necessary capital to exploit—"

"Yeah. I'll bet you might," High Pockets growled. "I reckoned that was what you was leadin' up to. Well, the answer's *no!* Miss Rosalee ain't partial to gettin' mixed up with snakes."

The gambler yanked his glance from the girl's white face. Plain wickedness was in the look he whipped at Hague. "Did I understand you—"

"If you didn't," High Pockets said, "I'm glad to repeat it. Miss Rosalee, I said, ain't partial to gettin' mixed up with snakes."

Frodsham's lids rolled lower; his eyes were very bright. He nodded slowly and a tight smile bent his lips. "I remember you now. You're the man that came pushing into my place yesterday and dragged off one of my guests."

He leaned a little forward. "I want to tell you something, Mister—" Discriminating belligerence showed in the twist of his lantern jaw. "I'd just like to advise you that people who put a value on their health don't talk that way to me. I'm not in the habit of making threats—"

"I'm not either," High Pockets snapped. "But it'll be to your advantage to get yourself beyond that wire about as quick as you are able!"

8

"I'LL BREAK THIS GODDAMN RAFTER!"

Frodsham's forehead puckered above the sandy brows that topped his eyes. The eyes themselves clung fixedly to High Pockets' face and in them could be seen a light of deepening interest. He did not at once take the curt advice Hague offered, but thrust his hands deep down inside the pockets of his blue serge coat. Teetering thus upon his bootheels a slow grin crossed his lips.

"I guess we understand each other," he remarked with a soft, cool chuckle.

"Yeah," Hague said. "I sabe *you* all right! You're out to get this ore any way you can."

"An' you figure to stop me, eh?"

"I may not stop you, but you'll get a hell of a run for your money."

The gambler appeared to think for a moment; to be scanning something in his mind. He said abruptly: "How about you and me getting together on this thing? Isn't there some way we could pool our interests and—"

"Other things aside," Hague said, "I ain't in the habit of poolin' anything with polecats."

"So I'm a polecat now. Aren't you sort of getting your animals mixed? Last time I was a snake." Frodsham's smile was easy, bland, suave; it was endowed with a placating quality—the kind of smile with which a patient elder might regard a fractious child.

"At least you'll hear my proposition, won't you?" He appealed to Rosalee, his long face shaped to the sad, wise look of a martyr.

The desire was strong in Hague to get from his horse and knock the fellow sprawling—to knock the goddamn impudence down his throat. But, checking the rush of his lifting temper, he curbed the impulse and held silent, waiting for Rosalee to speak.

Though the paleness was still upon her cheeks her chin came up. She said bluntly: "I will listen —though it won't be doing you the smallest amount of good. Mr. Hague is my range boss and I follow his advice in matters of this kind."

Frodsham looked from one to the other. A faintly amused smile tugged the corners of his lips. "Mr. Hague is favored," he observed, and for an instant a calculating gleam showed back of his eyes. Then the eyes were frisking a glance over Rosalee's wind-whipped figure.

"May I congratulate—?" he began, and stopped awkwardly as the hot bright color poured across her cheeks. "Er—pardon me. My mistake, I'm sure—I naturally thought . . ." He let the rest trail off and Tranch's lips curled in a sneer.

It was all High Pockets could do to keep from jerking the gun at his belt. The insinuation had been so smoothly carried off—so premeditatively deliberate.

He slid from his bronc with chalk-white cheeks.

The girl watched fascinated as Tranch began a nervous backing. She saw Frodsham turn with a surprise made very plausible. But it wasn't fooling Hague, nor stopping him. Grimly silent, shoulders stiffly swinging, he cut the distance between himself and Frodsham with a cold white fury blazing from his eyes.

She pressed the knuckles of one hand against her teeth, striving to choke back her fright. It was like something glimpsed in a nightmare, this mad advance of High Pockets against that grinning, unblinking gambler. She longed to cry out to him, to stop this dread advance before it culminated in something too terrible to be witnessed. She tried to shut her eyes but could not.

The harsh rasp of Hague's big spurs in the utter stillness was like the knell of doom.

She had never seen him look like this. There was a wild, primitive abandon in the swinging of those hips and shoulders and a fierce and ruthless implacability about the set of his cheeks that chilled her through and through.

Then suddenly he had stopped. He stood three feet from Frodsham with the gun in his belt untouched. The sulky brilliance of the gambler's eyes had deepened; his feet were planted wide apart, his upper body been a little forward.

"I'm going to beat the livin' daylights out of you." Hague spoke with a terrible, impelling earnestness. "Get set."

Rosalee saw the gambler's muscles leap and stiffen; saw his gun jump out with a speed that jammed her breath.

But, fast as the draw had been, she saw Hague catch the gambler's pistol by the barrel, wrench it savagely aside as flame burst from its muzzle, and drive a crashing right to Frodsham's jaw.

The gambler staggered, went reeling backward with a wild attempt to keep his balance, the gun left dangling in High Pockets' grasp. She saw High Pockets hurl the weapon from him and go slashing after Frodsham with a bitter oath.

The gambler, crouched, met the charge white-cheeked, both fists blurring. They drove High Pockets back a pace but did not stop him—hardly checked him. A long clean left to the gambler's chin exploded like a paper bag. Frodsham went back on his haunches and before he could collect himself, a slamming right spread-eagled him on the ground.

Dusty, disheveled, Frodsham clawed erect with grunted curses. They were like two beasts, snarling, growling, striving for the kill. Body struck body. The sound of that meaty impact sent a shiver down Rosalee's spine. When she could look again, Frodsham had both arms wrapped round High Pockets' torso and Hague's blurred fists were drumming the gambler's ribs.

She saw Frodsham break from the tough punishment gasping. Saw High Pockets, grimly following, bury a feint-distorted left to the wrist in the gambler's wheezing wind. She gasped herself in impulsive sympathy as Frodsham, doubled up, reeled away with a choking sob. High Pockets, springing forward, without mercy drove a blow to the side of Frodsham's head that put him sprawling in the dirt.

But Clayton Frodsham had been raised on this

kind of stuff. He lay still for several minutes not out but getting his breath back, striving to collect his half-dazed wits. He was not licked, but he was rapidly realizing the mistake of under-estimating this heavy-handed man from Texas. He got to his feet more slowly this time. There was respect and caution in the glance he whipped about him, in the way he stood with shoulders hunched while looking over the ground.

High Pockets said, "Get up your dukes—I ain't near done with you."

"Look out!" screamed a girl's scared voice.

Frodsham was coming at him when that desperate cry ripped through the hush. It swung High Pockets clear around. Even as he whirled a gun went off, its load just missing his shoulder. Flame stabbed outward from his hip. Gun thunder lashed the rocky slopes. Then Tranch, the gun sliding from his loosened grip, was lurching backward, sagging against the Tailbone wire with a twisted face gone white as wood-ash. The knees buckled beneath his weight, abruptly spilling him in the dust.

That much Hague saw—then something crashed against his head. Swift blackness blanked his vision, exploded in wheeling lights. The ground came up and slapped his face.

He was out, completely out for one brief fleeting moment. Then sight returned. Blurrily, through something that was like red mist but that High Pockets knew for blood, he saw Frodsham standing over him, roan cheeks aslant with triumph, a foot drawn back to boot him.

Cold fury rushed Hague to full consciousness.

He caught that grounded foot and tugged. Frodsham, jerked off balance, came down with a smothered curse. Dust bulged, and through it High Pockets saw the gambler coming at him, a clubbed six-shooter gripped in a bleeding fist. High Pockets, with a mighty effort, writhed aside as the gun descended, rolled clear and struggled to a knee.

Frodsham dropped the gun and lunged for him. Hague gained his feet but could not get clear of the battering slugging of the gambler's lancing fists. It was terrific punishment. Lurching, staggering, reeling, half-blinded, High Pockets continued backing from it.

"Bust 'im, Clay!" screamed a man's high voice. "Bust the livin' hell out of him!"

Another—some way reminiscent of Organ Smith's—snarled: "Smash his goddamn face off!"

And certainly Frodsham was doing his very best. Briefly, as wind tore gaps in the lifted dust, Hague caught blurred glimpses of townsmen hurrying across the flattened fence. But he had no time to wonder what had happened to the Rafter hands—it was all he could do to keep his feet under the pummeling bombardment of the gambler's flying blows.

Frodsham was grinning now, confident of victory.

There was no steam left in Hague's wild blows. Not more than one in ten was landing; these the gambler was shrugging off with taunting laughs. The boss of Silver City was enjoying himself.

Abruptly two quick hooks, violent, jolting, straightened High Pockets like a poker. He caught one dazed glimpse of Rosalee's white face, then was belting backward beneath a long range drive of the gambler's cutting right.

Hooked up in his spurs, he struck heavily against the shaley slope. He lay there, winded, battered, bleeding from a score of lacerations. He was pretty near through, and knew it. His arms were lumps of lead, his fists completely numb. The blinding pain in his head had destroyed that smooth coordination of mind and muscle that in the past had been his armor. Those reserves of strength built up by clean living were gone, exhausted. Frodsham's hammering fists had reduced him to a shattered hulk. But when, through blurring tears, he saw the gambler leaping at him, he roused to a final effort.

Perhaps it was that backdrop of gloating, tight-pinched faces that fanned the stubborn spark within him—perhaps it was the scared, white look of Rosalee.

A faint grin tugged his cracked and bloody lips. In that final moment when the leaping gambler, eager for the kill, was almost on him—so close that he could see the exultant savagery of Frodsham's tisted features—he brought his knees up level with his shoulders and kicked out. Those driving, booted feet took Frodsham squarely in the chest, smashing him backward, sending him sprawling, breathless, gasping, into the tight-packed ranks of the watchers.

Hague got a knee beneath him, shoved himself erect and stood there swaying, groggy, his battered face still bitter with the turbulence of these last minutes.

He made a dread and awesome figure with his patched shirt hanging in tatters from his bare and grit-smeared shoulders. His morose glance raked the silent, sullen watchers ringing Frodsham's prostrate body. They had no need to tell him this was not the end anticipated; it was patent in the rebellious detail of those darkened cheeks, in the tautened slant of wind-whipped features.

"Clear out," he said with his voice a husky rumble. He stretched a shaking arm to point across the trampled fence. "Clear out an' take that yellow cur with you—take that carrion, too," he directed, with a burning look at the crumpled Tranch.

The crowd started drifting toward the Rafter boundary. They went with wooden faces, making no comment.

High Pockets watched them, faintly rocking on his bootheels, face still warped by the turmoil he had come through. He watched a couple of bartenders lift Tranch by feet and shoulders, saw a sundry handful bend above the groaning Frodsham; heard the guarded mutter of a low-held conversation.

Talked sloughed off and the group went stiff as High Pockets joined in. Frodsham was on his feet and shaking his spare shoulders, twisting his head from side to side with a hand pressed against his chest. He looked still half dazed from his fall and from the shocking impact of Hague's spurred boots. He said: "Never mind the goddamn gun," and struck a man's extended hand away from him. "Tell Hague he ain't near seen the end of this—say I'll get him for this business if it's the last damned thing I do. Go tell him that."

High Pockets snapped his answer like a whip-lash. "I hear you, Frodsham. Get off of Rafter before you're ridden off on a rail."

Frodsham wheeled to drive his glance across the men's shoulders. A vengeful fury marked the slant of his lean roan cheeks. "By God," he said, "I'll break this goddam Rafter! You'll not get an ounce of that copper to a bank! Don't come whining round when the going starts getting rough—you nor any of your men! I'll show you what it means to cross Clay Frodsham!"

9

THE SHERIFF HANDS OUT SOME ADVICE

Through the night Hague sat hunkered on his bootheels with a cold pipe gripped between his teeth and from the obscurity of a live-oak thicket watched the glow of distant campfires. Why was it that the melody of a woman's voice was able so to touch him—to stir him as did Rosalee's? Why was it that those things a man most searched for were denied him? Why was life such a complex pattern?

Down there about those campfires beyond the restrung Tailbone Rafter wire was Frodsham's crew from Silver. All up and down the base of the slope they'd staked out claims in the Forest. More than one burly fellow had attempted to stake higher ground, but had been turned back by Rafter rifles; there was no high ground along the boundary that had been left open—Hague had seen to that before the crowd from Silver landed.

But the situation, as he knew, was ever changing. All night long newcomers from remoter regions had been steadily trickling in, augmenting Frodsham's camp in the hollow. Bobbing lanterns down there showed where tents were going up among the tangle of crowded wagons. Fires and lanterns now were dotting the flat for half a mile; and by dawn men would probably be camped clear over across the hogback. The Rafter hands were taking their sleep in shifts, three rifles ever ready to check a rush. But how much longer, Hague wondered grimly, would the mere brandishing of weapons prove any protection?

The situation was rapidly growing critical. Rafter's balance of power, with all these new men trickling in, must prove of short duration unless he pulled more men from the ranch or put new men on the payroll. This was going to be the old story of the haves against the have-nots, he thought bitterly. Unless some of that crowd down yonder struck ore, or at least found trace of color to give them hope, it could be only a question of time till everyone not working for Rafter would be solidly back of Frodsham.

Hague sucked his pipe with thoughts turned dour.

Rosalee's remarks before she left came back to him. "Must this sort of thing go on?" she'd asked resentfully, referring to his fight with Frodsham. "*Must* it?" She'd looked up at him fiercely, stormy eyes rebellious. "Better to sell this mine right now—*at once,* than be the cause of any more men dying!"

He'd tried to reason with her, to show her that no matter who had deed to the Copper Girl, the forward march of events could not be checked. Mining camps, he'd reminded her, were hell; these things followed patterns that were beyond the power of man to change. Human nature being what it was, of what avail could be her selling of the Copper Girl—to Frodsham or to anyone else? These fights, these brawls and shootings would go on just the same, he'd pointed out.

"Maybe so," she'd said; "but they'd not be on *my* conscience."

"They're not on your conscience now," he'd told her. "I'm managing your affairs—I'm the one the blame will fall on. Look here, ma'am. There's just two sides to this affair, the right side an' the wrong. You represent the right. You own this land; the only ore in sight is on it. If we had any decent law in this man's country, you'd have it back of you. Since the only law we've got will be bought by Frodsham and his crowd, we've got to revert to the only kind of law that's left—the kind promoted by a pistol. This is a hard tough land and we're living in a hard tough age; it has been my experience that only the quick and the strong survive. Unless you care to pull down the flag and turn your property over to Frodsham and his wolves, you've got to fight!"

He'd told her this truth vehemently, endeavoring to show her where she stood. "D'you think your Dad would have turned his holdings over to that polecat bunch of cutthroats?" She had not answered. Rebellious and resentful, she had eyed him bitterly—as though he represented personally all these things that were proving so distasteful. She had not answered; she had gone off without saying anything, but leaving him in charge.

He thought of his reason for coming here, of his long hard search for peace. There'd be no peace here for him; the enemies he'd made already

would see to that. In the darkness High Pockets'
grin was twisted bleak. He still could strap a
saddle on his roan, could ride on out of the
country.

But he knew in his heart he wouldn't.

Clayton Frodsham was in a mood. Scarred
hands thrust deep down in his coat pockets, he
was savagely pacing his back-room office, five
strides this way, five strides that, the fury of his
late encounter with Hague still twisting his florid
features. It had been the act of a fool, his tangling
with the Tailbone Rafter foreman this noon. He
could see that now. But Tranch had been so
damnably sure! He'd called the play *easy as
rollin' off a log;* and then, with everything
working in his favor, he'd muffed it and got himself killed.

Trouble was, they'd underestimated this cocky
Texas rooster. In spite of Ballard's report, and
the recent evidence of their own eyes, they'd not
believed any man could be so goddam quick with
a gun! It was incredible! It made Frodsham's
flesh crawl just to think about it—but, mostly, it
made him mad. He had never suffered in his life
as he had suffered today at High Pockets' hands.
His loss in prestige was incalculable. If he'd had
the wit to quit when the fellow shot Tranch—

But no; his greatest mistake had been in with-
drawing from the Gap leaving Hague alive and in
charge. *That* was the biggest boner—he should
have killed the outlander then and there. Instead,
he'd ranted threats like the cheap tinhorn Hague
had called him, and had come away.

There must be no more such blunders. This

thing must be thought out carefully; success had turned him careless and another such slip must result in definite loss of power. There was far too much at stake to let one man—

Someone was knocking on the door. With a smothered oath Frodsham wheeled his spare form round and yanked it open. A gust of sound poured in, tobacco haze, the reek of whisky and unwashed bodies. One of his bartenders stood there, muttering apologetically, explaining that young Tommy Parshall had just come in and was very anxious to see him. "He's lookin' right urgent, Clay—sure in a sweat about somethin'."

Frodsham ran a practiced eye across the three-deep crowd that bellied his long sleek bar. A big night; every gambling layout was crammed. Abruptly he ironed the scowl from his face and nodded. "All right, Joe. Send him in. And if you see Abe Klarson round anyplace, send him in, too. I'd like to see him before young Parshall leaves."

Back inside the office again, Frodsham seated himself at his desk and began sorting through the accumulated stack of papers that littered its surface. Back under the pigeonholes a long narrow mirror was tilted in such a way that, though he had his back to the door, he could see anyone who entered and could keep them in view without appearing to do so. He had learned the value of keeping folks waiting.

When someone presently knocked, he said "Come in," without turning around, and continued thumbing his papers for five minutes after young Parshall had entered. The kid had something on his mind all right; his face was flushed and his eyes kept jumping round nervously. He growled abruptly: "For Chrissake, Clay—"

Frodsham swung round in his chair with a look of impatience.

He said with a fine air of exasperation: "What is it this time, Bumpaw?" and took a vindictive satisfaction at the scowl with which the youth received the hated nickname. "Can't you see I'm busy? You know this is payday night for the mines and—" He broke off to pause, and eyed the flushed young man intently. "Oh," he said as though mollified. "Came to pay off those IOU's, eh?"

Young Parshall's scowl bit deeper. Resentment tinged his words. "You know damn well I ain't got the money—"

"Ain't got it? Didn't I tell you tomorrow was the deadline?" Frodsham looked at him sternly. "You're a damn risky business, kid, and I've been pretty patient. I told you yesterday I'd have to have that money, and you said you'd get it."

Young Tommy squirmed. "Rosalee wouldn't give it to me—and she's thrown away the last money she intends to on my gambling. What the hell's all the rush?"

"You call it rush, do you?" asked the gambler, eyeing him grimly. "What do you think I pay *my* debts with?—your IOU's? It takes a lot of money to run a place like this. Hundreds of dollars change hands every night, and on paydays—"

"I'm no range tramp! You'll get your money. You know—"

"I know I better get it by tomorrow night," said Frodsham quietly. "I'm a pretty good fellow up to a certain point; but I've no intention of being strung along for years. That hundred thousand your old man put in trust for you don't mature for another three years and I'm not waiting that long. I was speaking to Abe Klarson about it yesterday and he tells me—" Frodsham broke off as an authoritative thumping banged the door. "Come in!" he said, and a square-jawed man with a toothpick thrust in one corner of his tight-lipped mouth came in and shut the door. Lamplight skittered from the star on his cowhide vest.

Young Tommy's cheeks went white as paint as his scared eyes met this fellow's glance.

"Howdy, Klarson," Frodsham said. "You come at a most opportune time. You've met young Parshall, haven't you? No? Well, this is him—kid brother to the girl that's running Rafter. Shake hands with Sheriff Klarson, Tommy."

In a daze young Parshall put a nervous hand out. Klarson looked him over without charity, glanced at the hand and spat. "This the fella that's tryin' to get out of payin' his honest debts?"

"Well, I wouldn't put it quite that strong," said Frodsham, frowning. "He says he aims to pay them. But he hasn't any ready cash."

The sheriff surveyed the youngster coldly, dark eyes boring into him. "How much does he owe you, Frodsham?"

"Let's see," said the gambler thoughtfully. "I've got a memorandum of it 'round here someplace." He leafed through the papers on his desk. "Here it is. Sixty-five eighty."

"Sixty-five dollars an'—?"

"Sixty-five *hundred* and eighty dollars," corrected Frodsham.

Klarson said coldly: "That's a hell of a lot of money."

"I can pay it," cried Tommy, desperate. "All I need is a little time. He never told me he was in a hurry—"

"What have you got to secure this money?"

"Just his promissory notes," Frodsham said with a shrug.

The sheriff nodded. "Well, we might get a lien—"

"I've got a hundred-thousand dollar trust fund—"

"That won't be touchable for another three years," cut in the gambler. "I need that money now. I've given him till tomorrow night to get it," he explained to the sheriff.

"My advice to you is to get it," Klarson told young Tommy grimly. He looked at Frodsham. "I'll see Judge Towner in the meantime an' get the papers fixed up in case this kid reneges—"

"Well, I don't want to be too hard on him," Frodsham murmured.

The sheriff scowled. "That's what's the matter with people like him. Folks lend 'em money an' then are too soft-hearted to do anything about it when they don't pay up. Things are goin' to be different hereafter. There's been a new law passed this month with regard to matters of this kind. Afraid it's out of your hands now, Frodsham. You've given him till tomorrow night, so we'll let it go that long. After that, however—" He left the rest unfinished and looked at Tommy significantly. "I'd get the money if I were you."

10

WOLF'S CANDLE

After Tommy, with a face showing belated realization of his folly, had taken his departure, the sheriff and the gambler exchanged appraising glances. Frodsham, smiling coldly, crossed to the safe, pulled open the door and removed from its dark interior a packet of thin, crisp, oblong papers. He handed this to Klarson and stood silent while the sheriff thumbed its edges. Klarson looked up with a grunt.

"You goin' tight on me?"

"Not tight," replied Frodsham meaningly, "—just cautious. You'll get the rest when the deal's wound up. Now look here," he said, and lowered his voice. "I've got another job you can handle and I don't wany any slips." He talked rapidly for five minutes, and when he had concluded the sheriff whistled. He looked at Frodsham dubiously. "Be pretty risky, won't it?"

"D'you think I'm paying you to put a shine on the seat of your pants?"

"I know damn well you ain't. But I'm in this thing for money same as the rest of you. I like to know I'm going to be round to collect it when the time comes. I'll do this for you, Clay, but—"

"You'll do it," said Frodsham curtly, "and there won't be any buts. You know what you've got at stake. Get goin'."

The sheriff regarded him a moment longer, and then with a sour smile walked through the door.

Frodsham gave the man time to get out of the building, then set a thumb down heavily on a button. The head barman entered with a question in his eyes. "Joe," said Frodsham grimly, "I want Ballard, Smith and Caprosa. Send them back here right away. Send Yuma Taiban back here, too."

When the four men filed into the office Frodsham raked them with a quick, hard glance. He nodded to Taiban to close the door, then started talking.

It was 3 A.M. by the clock on Frodsham's desk when he let them out. He regarded the clock with a cool remote smile as he husked a cigar from its wrapper, bit off an end and placed it in his mouth. He was reaching for his coat when he heard the door close softly in back of him. He did not whirl as another man might have done; he'd lived too long in mining camps to make a mistake like that. He picked up the coat, slipped his spare shoulders into it, when finally he did turn round, took care to make the movement casual. He showed no surprise when he saw young Parshall facing him above a gun.

There was a jerky, harried look in Tommy's eyes. His lips were twitching. He said huskily: "I want those papers, Clay."

"Papers? Which papers, Tommy?"

"You know which ones. God damn you, Clay—don't stall!"

Clayton Frodsham held a lighted match to the end of his cigar, puffed several times and said: "You mean those IOU's?"

"Yes!" Tommy's hand was shaking. "I'll not be pushed any further, Clay. You'd better get them—quick!"

Young Parshall was plainly too high-strung to be anything but in earnest. Yet the gambler showed no sign of alarm. Removing the cigar from his mouth, he stood a moment in thoughtful contemplation of its glowing end. He said quietly then, "Of course you know what you're doing, Tommy. You realize that if I hand you what you're asking for, it's going to make an outlaw—"

"Never mind that! Choke off the blat an' get those papers!" Tommy snarled. "Get 'em quick or as God's my witness, Clay, I'm going to shoot!"

The gambler's lips curled back in a sneer. "Don't try to run that bluff on me; you haven't got the nerve to shoot—you couldn't stand the thought of getting your neck stretched for it afterwards. Now put up that gun before somebody comes in and sees you. Look here; let's talk this over sensibly. Let's talk this over as one man to another—"

"It's a little late for talkin', Clay. You told me if I'd help you out with that copper deal you'd forget those IOU's. Then yesterday you said I'd have to get the money; tonight you brought Abe Klarson into it." His voice rose bitterly, dangerously. "I can't trust you, Clay! You goin' to get those notes or ain't you?"

"No," said the gambler flatly. "Now go ahead an'—*Grab 'im, Ballard!*"

Tommy whirled.

There was no one back of him. Before he could turn again Frodsham had him in a grip of steel. There was a quick, sharp wrench and the pistol skittered across the floor.

The gambler stepped back, letting go his hold.

"Damn you, Frodsham!" Tommy sobbed.

"Listen a minute, you brash young fool! There's one way you can get out of this—just one. If you want to keep out of jail, go draw a check on the ranch account. I've got to have that money by tomorrow night!"

"But—but my sister signs the ranch account—"

"What of it? You can work a pen, can't you?"

Tommy stared, white-lipped, incredulous. "Are you suggesting that I *forge*—?"

"Don't put those words in my mouth," snapped Frodsham sharply. "I'm not suggesting anything. I'm simply trying to show you where you stand. Pick up that gun now and get out of here."

Tommy still hung moveless, staring. The tongue he passed over parched lips did not wet them. "God, Clay! I—I couldn't do a thing like that!"

"No one's asking you to," replied the gambler coldly. "All I'm interested in is getting my money back. Come on now, hop it. I've got to get to bed."

Tommy shuddered. Like a man gone blind he groped his way to the gun and picked it up.

Ten minutes later Frodsham turned out the lamp and left his office by a door that gave into an alley. One more move and the chain of events he was setting in motion would be complete. Turning his hatbrim down across his eyes, he headed for Texas Street where the lights of cribs and sporting houses colored the shadows red.

11

"DEAD AS A GODDAM DOORNAIL!"

It was 4:20 when High Pockets rose in the faint
half-light preceding dawn and stretched the kinks
from muscles cramped by the movelessness of his
long vigil. He rose with an unpleasant realization:
He was no longer his own master. He'd worked
for other people in the past, but with certain stip-
ulations, certain conditions that gave him run of
the range. This wasn't quite the same. He was
boss of Rafter, yes; but he was accountable to
Rosalee, and the thought was cramping. It was a
hamper on initiative. It turned him restless, dis-
satisfied, doubtful if he could meet this coming
turbulence in a way that she'd approve. In the
past he'd always seen conditions had been such
that he could quit, could pull his pin and drift
when things were not to his liking. But this was
different. She was a woman and he could not
leave her to face this thing alone. Yet already she
was chafing. She could not approve his handling
of Clayton Frodsham; and the quick, sure manner
in which retribution had overtaken Tranch
appeared to have filled her with resentment. They

took a different view of things, this girl and Hague; and this disparity, he saw, was bound to cause increasing friction. It was not that he held any brief for violence—all his instincts were against it. But there were times when and places where only violence, swift and furious, could avail against the schemes and trickery of certain people; and he had lived too long among their kind to be in any doubt of this.

Hague was afraid, and his fears were mounting. As he saw conditions, there could be but—

He cut loose of the unwelcome conviction, and with a mouth gone grim and clamped, ducked under the Rafter wire and strode to where his men stood guard with rifles.

"I want Gene Duncan," he said curtly, and one of the boys stepped off to wake him.

Duncan, rubbing the sleep from his eyes, came over and Hague took him away to one side. Without preliminary he said quietly: "We're pretty much up against it, Gene. Our hand is going to be forced. We've got to have men to work this mine; to open it up. We've got to have others to keep it going. I'm going to hire miners from that crowd down yonder." He stared morosely across the hollow where the lights of the copper stampeders winked like fireflies through the gloom.

"I've got to hire those men, but I can't trust them. Where can I get mercenaries to keep them straight and to keep the rest of 'em off?"

Gene Duncan shoved back his hat and scratched his head with a little grin. "Tough situation, ain't it?" He thought awhile. "There's some boys around this country you could probably hire all right. Question is, could we depend on 'em. If the goin' starts gettin' rough, they'll likely rattle their hocks an' high-tail it for the tules."

"We'll have to chance that part, I reckon. Who are these fellows you've got in mind?"

"Well," said Duncan consideringly, "there's the Lunkan boys, for instance—Washout an' Kettle-Belly Lunkan. They're a couple squatters that's got a haywire spread up Pinnywinkle Canyon. They sleep on the floor with newspapers wrapped around 'em account of they're too plain lazy to build 'em bunks an' too fool broke to buy any blankets. But they're fair to middlin' reliable if you make the price accommodatin'. Then there's eight or ten other nesters shacked up in these mountains that could be bought, if you had the price an' was willin' to guarantee 'em protection case they got in trouble."

Hague made up his mind. "Go get 'em," he said shortly, and turned away to get his horse.

Five minutes later he was riding down the slope to where the breakfast smells of cooking prospectors proved the treasure-seekers' camp astir.

He drifted round among the lanterns and camp-fires that dotted the pocket and were intermingled with jammed-up wagons and hobbled horses. The copper hunters were a mixed and sundry lot. Well-dressed merchants and gamblers immaculate in string ties, black frock coats and varied trousers brushed elbows with bearded ruffians, beady-eyed touts and tobacco-chewing teamsters in sweaty, grime-soiled clothing. Here and there, ignoring the hostile looks directed at him, Hague found red-shirted Cousin Jacks; these he hired wherever found until he had a good round twenty of them joking at his back.

"Here's the ledge, boys," he told them when they stood inside the Rafter wire. "You know the pay and you're guaranteed protection while you're on the job. McPherson, you're the boss. Get goin'."

He left them and went back among the trees and put his back against one while he rolled himself a smoke. He left his horse under saddle, not knowing when he might be needed. No fresh trouble so far, but there would be soon enough and it was well to be prepared. Frodsham would not sit back and wait for opportunity; he'd make his own opportunity and push it to the limit. Hague had dealt with men like Frodsham in the past and knew their caliber. He surmised the boss of Silver would already have put a price upon his pelt in hopes of speeding up things. Not that this unduly worried him; he had had this happen before and was well aware that eternal care and vigilance must be the cost he paid for health. But it made things a little harder.

At four in the afternoon, with the baked earth hot and shimmering, Gene Duncan came through the Gap with eight men riding after him. They pulled their horses up by Hague and introductions followed. These were the squatting, small-spread cowmen Duncan had gone for. Hague gave them a little talk. With sharps and Winchesters gleamingly cradled in their arms, they spread about and loafed in what shade offered.

When McPherson's men knocked off at seven o'clock two pole cabins had been erected—one for a bunkhouse and one for an office—and a vast pile of yellow earth had appeared to one side of where twenty feet of ledge lay exposed and gleaming in the shafts of the dying sun. No trouble had been thus far encountered with the Frodsham crowd from Silver, but the limits of their camp had crawled beyond the hogback and the sound of its presence was a constant, vibrant thing.

Supplies had come in from the ranch and more were on their way from Silver. Kettle-Belly Lunkan was busy above a fire with pots and pans and the rifle-toting squatters stood round him to a man, lightening his task with ready wit and free advice.

Kettle-Belly had the tailgate of his wagon down and was mixing up some batter when a couple of the Rafter boys came drifting over from their claims. "Holy cow, Gene! Is—is that a man?" one asked the other with astonishment spread thick upon his voice.

"You mean that pelican in the floursack apron? The bird that's makin' them dough-gods? Sure," Gene said reassuringly; "leastways—"

"Why, he ain't got no more hair'n a picked brand!" exclaimed the other, and some of the squatters snickered.

"I know," admitted Gene. "He looks about as useful as a twenty-two cartridge in a eight-gauge shotgun, but—"

"See here, boys," Kettle Belly said, turning around and slipping his belt a couple notches the better to display his unusual contour—or, perhaps, to give it elbow room. "That ain't no kind of way to talk at a cook. You ort to treat me

94

good. I hear that belly-cheater you got over at Rafter—"

"Don't mention him," muttered Duncan. "I can't abide his name."

"Is it true," Kettle-Belly asked, "that he's been feedin' you-alls salt pork so long that Ballard began sweatin' straight leaf lard an' his hide got so tarnation slick Miz Rosalee had to let 'im go for fear he couldn't hold his clothes on?"

Duncan's cheeks got a little red and the gathered squatters guffawed.

"You know, Gene," Kettle-Belly said, "some fella was tellin' me the other day about *your* case. This person said you wa'n't far behind Mister Ballard. He said you'd et so dang much chuck-wagon chicken you was gruntin' in your sleep an' was scared t' look f' fear you'd done sprouted a curly tail. Anythin' to it?"

While Duncan was scrooching down in his boots and wishing himself elsewhere, his companion, stretching his neck a bit, said: "Them saddle blankets you're shakin' up in that pail?"

"Well, yes," the cook said reflectively. "Some folks call 'em batter cakes, but I reckon you've hit it close enough. I figgered to throw in a little fried chicken so's to make you boys feel at home; an' then to top it off I thought mebbe we could have a few whistle berries. I was kinda hopin' we might have a little District Attorney on the side. But don't go daunsy—I'm fixin' up a special dish for you."

Duncan's companion made haste to change the subject. "Where's your band wagon, Kettle? I heard you was hubbin' it round the hills peddlin' stirrup leathers, straps, clothes an' all sorts of miscellaneous wonders."

"That's right," Kettle-Belly saidd. "An' this here's the very wagon—I just remodeled 'er a mite for this occasion."

"That your bone-rack over there," said the cowboy, pointing to an old and shad-bellied plug that looked about ready for the glue factory. The rotund gentleman in the floursack apron nodded. "Yep," he said. "A dang fine hoss for—"

"Looks to me," broke in the rider, "like the ol' scow's really dead but too chuckle-headed to lay down."

"Sure—" piped up Gene Duncan, "that's the buzzard bait Ol' Man Lusk jiggered that time the brockle-faced bull took after him!"

"All right, boys. All right," Kettle-Belly said good-naturedly. "A joke's a joke. But even a good one can be carried too far, as A'nt Fanny once remarked when her Guernsey heifer mistook her for the salt."

The chorus of guffaws snapped short when a rataplan of hurrying hoofs burst larruping from the rockribbed Gap. Every man turned round to stare.

Sun's last rays put a coating of brass against the Gap's far wall. Against this glare a bent-forward rider suddenly showed. A moment later this man came bursting from the purple shadows cast by a thicket of squatting cedars and yanked his bronc back on its haunches beside the wagon.

It was Bill Janes.

"Where's High Pockets?" His voice was urgent.

Duncan pointed and Janes whirled his horse in that direction.

The rifle-toting squatters exchanged significant glances. All had seen how the animal's sweat had lathered like razor soap about the edges of the blanket beneath Janes' saddle.

Hague's look was quick and hard. "What's wrong?" he said as Janes pulled up beside him.

"County recorder ain't been in his office all day," Janes answered, mopping the sweat from his face. "Couldn't find him round town anyplace, either. An' his office is plumb locked up."

Hague stared off across the widespread camp in the hollow.

"He ain't down there," Janes said. "He was in town last night—up till three-fifteen anyways. Three-four fellas remembered seein' him playin' poker at the Red Onion. But look—"

"You still got them location—?"

"Sure! But listen—get set for trouble now: Young Parshall was found in a back alley this noon—dead as a goddam doornail!"

12

A GHOST THAT WALKED

Hague stood for a long time staring off into the dusk. The curdled shadows were alive with memories, mocking him, calling him back. To him this swirling gloom was a crouched thing, stifling, monstrous, waiting to pounce and grab him.

He saw a great truth suddenly: No man could run from the past or put his destiny aside. The remembered curve of a cool, smooth cheek—a girl's eyes mutely pleading, was all too poignant; the recalled twist of a dying man's features remained too vivid. A man might escape many things, but he could not escape memory, nor could mere flight rub the pattern out.

Slaughter, rapine, ravishment lurked among these thickening shadows. Violence and malevolence still rode in strong high saddles; and though the cards had again been shuffled and redealt, this new hand was little different from the old. Turbulence was bright on all these watching faces. Bitterness was like a poison in his blood.

This was the old, the remembered pattern; it

was like a doom laid on him—like a curse.

Perhaps it was the way he stood gave the forward throw to his lean dark jaw. Upper body held stiffly canted, he raked Bill Janes with a searching look.

"Murder?"

"Well, that's the hell of it," Janes said grumpily. "I don't know. You'd think it was, the way they found him. Still an' all, I'd hate to say so. There was a six-gun on the ground beside him —you could see where it had struck when he let go of it. There was one empty shell in the cylinder an' one bullet hole in Tommy. He got it in the heart. Dead center."

He looked at Hague a moment thoughtfully. "It coulda been suicide." He said reluctantly: "There was powder burns upon his shirt."

"Let's take it from the start," Hague said. "You got to town. What time?"

"I dunno. Close to grub time—can say that much. Call it five. I had in mind what you had told me; was aimin' to record them notices an' start right back." He added virtuously: "Wasn't even figurin' to stop for a drink. Wasn't nobody in the recorder's office, though. I guessed he'd gone to supper an' got a bite myself. His place was shut up when I got back. I knew he'd be in town someplace. Startin' with them joints on Texas Street, I went through every saloon in town."

"What time did you hit the Red Onion?"

"Some time after three. I went there last—I hadn't any reason," he said defensively, "to suppose him an' Frodsham was feelin' chummy. They locked horns one time las' spring—"

99

"Get on with it," Hague grunted.

"Well, in Frodsham's place two-three fellas remembered seein' Taiban—that's the recorder's name—a bit earlier in the evenin'. Said they guessed he'd gone home to bed; said he wasn't any night owl, an' kinda laughed a little." Janes paused, seemed to be scanning something in his mind. He said: "I didn't think much about it then, but later I got to wonderin' if mebbe Frodsham hadn't put a spoke in Taiban's wheel—"

"You mean," said Hague, "that maybe Frodsham had him spirited off or somethin'?"

Janes nodded. "There's something screwy about that deal. I went out in the cactus a ways an' took myself forty winks. I was at that office at six A.M.—camped right down on the doorstep till after eleven. It was still closed when I hunted up Abe Klarson. Klarson's the sheriff. He didn't seem to know much about it; said mebbe Taiban had gone over to see his ol' man over round Chloride Flats someplace. While we were talkin', some tout from the Golden Goose come up an' said young Parshall had just been found in a back alley off of Texas Street.

"We went right over—that is, the sheriff did, an' I stuck with him. Parshall was layin' there with his face in the dirt an' his gun just a little to one side of him. There was dirt plugged in the muzzle and a mark on the ground showin' where it hit when he dropped it. One cartridge, like I said, had been shot off."

"Klarson make any inquiries about where Tommy had been?"

"Yeah; he made a few. Seemed to know pretty near as much about it though as anyone. Seems like he'd been talkin' with Tommy an' Frodsham last night in Frodsham's office. ᵀ—"

"What about?" Hague cut in softly.

"He didn't mention. Kind of shied away from it. I don't reckon," Janes said consideringly, "it was anything would get him extra votes. After I'd helped Klarson get Tommy to Doc Johnston's, I got my horse an' lit a shuck. I figured you'd be wantin' to know." He looked over toward the wagon. "Lunkan got any grub left?"

Hague didn't answer; his cheeks were warped with thinking.

It looked very much like this second round was going to go to Frodsham. He did not put any great stock in that tale of the recorder's sudden trip to Chloride Flats to see his father. Taiban had been got at; either Frodsham had managed to bribe him, or had got some bucko to snake the man out of town. That talk Frodsham had had with the Sheriff and Tommy didn't look too damned good, either. There was something kind of smelly about that talk, coming as it had just before young Parshall's death.

Tommy *might* have committed suicide; but High Pockets didn't think so. He didn't believe that Rosalee's brother had had that much cold nerve.

It seemed to him that Tommy's death and this business of the vanishing recorder were too much of a type. Too definitely slanted. This was Frodsham's way of pulling him into town; this was what the gambler had done to make certain Hague would come.

"Let's have them notices," he said to Janes.

And, when the puncher had given them to him, he smiled with his teeth and climbed up into the saddle.

If town was where they wanted him, they should not be disappointed.

It was this swift-flaring rage and intense love of justice that in the past had brought Hague most of his trouble. Enemies were quick to read a weakness into High Pockets' reckless temper and to use it as a lever to their advantage. And they were more than halfway right. It *was* a weakness and, given proper insight, could be used as a lever. Few, however, had been the persons who could boast having used it that way long.

None of these were boasting now.

It was a weakness just the same, though, as High Pockets had been made aware. Under certain circumstances, as now, he was powerless to curb that wickedly mounting rage—that desire to rip and smash and batter, but he was far from being without cognizance of its danger. He might scorn the sneaking tactics of treacherous schemers such as Frodsham, but he'd no intention of strolling into their dens without his wits about him.

He rode clear-thinkingly alert, well realizing the possibilities of ambush. He rode with keen eyes raking the curdled dusk and with a heavy carbine slung beneath his leg.

There were several angles to this business that was taking him to Silver; and there were several hombres likely hanging round, who would give considerable to see him planted with his boots on. For instance Ballard, and that little swart-faced foreigner he'd disarmed with a hasty shot that day he'd gone in after Tommy. Organ Smith would not be pulling any punches, either, if he saw a chance to do him in without too much risk to himself.

Hague shrugged these thoughts away from him. He'd lived too long with danger to start getting nervous now. Regardless of this rage that roweled him, he knew what he was after; he saw the issues that were at stake with a clarity that would have amazed the unscrupulous boss of Silver. He saw several of the moves Clayton Frodsham was bound to make, and they did not improve his temper any more than Tommy's death had done. He cared nothing for Tommy personally; it was the effect his death might have on Rosalee that bothered him.

He thought of what Bill Janes had told him, of the matter of that gun. There was a thing about that weapon that he meant to know, and when he learned, a lot might be explained.

He wondered what Tommy, Frodsham and the sheriff had found to talk about last night. That the conversation had had its part in Tommy's sudden passing he could not doubt.

It was a little after one when he reached Silver. Things were going strong and light from swinging doors and windows threw its yellow bars across the road.

Tugging his hat a little lower he racked his roan before the Sheriff's office and, swinging down, stood by it for a moment thinking. Then he strode on in, not bothering to knock.

"You the Sheriff of these parts?" he asked the fellow eyeing him across the desk.

"Yeah. Klarson is the name. You lookin' for me?"

"Not exactly. I'm looking for a gun—the one you found beside young Parshall this mornin'."

Klarson looked him over carefully.

This sheriff, Hague observed, was a blocky-looking fellow with a great wide forehead and penetrating eyes. His smoke-gray glance was taking High Pockets in methodically; and back of it, Hague saw, there was an alert, uneasy speculation.

"Young Parshall's gun, eh?" he said softly. "What's your interest in it?"

"The gun that was found beside him here this mornin'," Hague corrected.

"You think there's any difference?"

"Quien sabe. I'd like to have a look at it. Any objection?"

The sheriff's smoky gaze roved his scantily-furnished office with a queer restlessness, wheeled round at last again to fix his visitor with that odd considering attention, but now there was a new light flickering in its depths and it took especial notice of the gun butt protruding from the waistband of High Pockets' belted Levis.

"Who you been fightin' with?" he asked.

"I can't see," High Pockets told him, "that it's any of your business."

The sheriff seemed to reflect on this awhile. Still thinking, he got out his makings and rolled another monument to Durham. He struck a match and across the smoke he put between them said: "I might make that same remark about this gun you're huntin'."

"Are you goin' to?"

"I haven't quite decided," Klarson said. Then, abruptly nodding as though to something in his mind, he tucked the cigarette in one corner of his tight-lipped mouth, shoved back his chair and, bending forward, pulled open a drawer a little way and took from it a forty-five caliber Colt's pistol. He studied Hague from squinted eyes as, butt forward, he pushed the weapon toward him.

"This just the way you found it?"

The sheriff nodded.

High Pockets picked up the pistol, twirled the cylinder experimentally and shook the fired shell into his palm. He studied it a moment, eyed the sheriff and replaced it. "Got a toothpick handy?"

Klarson dug one from his vest, watching intently as Hague removed the dirt from the gun's plugged muzzle. "I hadn't ought to let you do that," he remarked. "You might be destroying evidence."

High Pockets looked at him derisively. "That supposed to be a joke?"

Klarson didn't answer. He was watching Hague squint down the weapon's barrel.

When High Pockets had done with his examination and without comment had put the gun down on the desk, change had subtly altered the set of Klarson's features. "Pretty thorough, aren't you?"

"It pays to be," Hague said, and looked him in the eye. "You're sure this is Parshall's gun?"

"I'm not sure—no," the sheriff answered carefully. "I did presume so, since it's the one we found beside him, but—" He let the rest trail off, raising his left hand casually, slowly rasped his jaw while his hard eyes searched High Pockets' face. "I can see you've made a discovery. Mind tellin' me what it is?"

"I've found," Hague told him softly, "that this gun has not been fired."

Tight silence closed around them.

Klarson said abruptly: "Are you hintin'—?"

"I'm not hinting anything. I'm tellin' you a fact."

The sheriff's gaze beat hard against High Pockets' face. "Then suppose you tell me another. I've been pretty obligin' in this matter. Suppose you favor me a little. I'd like to know your interest."

A faint smile crossed High Pockets' lips. There was no mirth in it. "I'm the Tailbone Rafter foreman," he said softly. "The name is Hague—High Pockets Hague."

The sheriff's still attention held a cold and wicked look. Several moments passed without any contribution from him. Then: "You can close the door behind you when you leave."

Hague climbed stiffly into the saddle and turned his bronc for a slow and thoughtful glance across the town. Then, building himself a smoke, he let the animal pick its way down Broadway's hill, cynosure for the curious stares of those who loafed along the warped plank walks and lounged among the store-front shadows.

He felt abruptly old and worn, more than ever weary of his lot and of the long hard search for a peace he could not find. So much had happened since that day when in a burst of powdersmoke he had settled for once and all the score with Long Joe Branton, besmircher of his father's name. So much had happened, yet so little that had been of benefit. He wondered if all his life he would be fighting others' battles.

It was a close and sultry night—unusual in this high country. Hardly a breeze stirred the hock-deep dust to Silver's streets and the occasional oaks that along this road traced foliage against the stars showed not the faintest quiver.

He reached the bottom of the hill and turned his roan to the right on Bullard Street, idly wondering what men found to recompense lives wasted in a town.

He was fourteen feet from the Red Onion's front when swift flexure of his knees put a stop to the roan's tired plodding.

A bar of light thrown outward from a window by some obscure shifting of the men beyond that moment cleaved the mealy blackness like a spot-light. Caught in the center of this shaft, on the walk outside and obviously heading for the entrance, was a thickset man whose cream-colored Stetson was shoved far back from his forehead. A livid scar showed plain there for a moment—a mark Hague knew and recognized, for he had been the cause of it.

He sat the saddle stiffly with his tough and rugged face gone wooden, watching the half-leaf doors swing shut behind a man he'd left for dead in Alamo—the brother of Joe Branton.

13

THE BAITED TRAP

High Pockets wasted no time in footless conjecture, but followed the man on in. Not immediately, but soon enough so that in case the fellow had got a look at him he'd drawn no wrong conclusions.

Nerves taut, face blank as pounded metal, he put his back against a wall and raked the smoky room with eyes that missed no slightest detail. Branton had his back to him, watching a hand of poker; there were not many other customers in the place. Only four men were draped along the mahogany. A hunch came to High Pockets suddenly and he beckoned the bartender over.

"What's up?"

The barman shrugged. "Damn town's about wound up, if you're askin' me. Everybody's cut for Bonanza—gettin' ready to pull out ourselfs. What'll you have? Rye or bourbon?"

"Where's Bonanza?"

"Ain't you—?" began the man and stopped as Joe, the head barkeep came trotting over, motioning him away. "Evenin', Mister Hague," Joe said. "What can we do for you?"

"You can supply me with a little information," Hague said grimly. "I understand you're movin' to Bonanza—that what they're callin' the camp beyond our boundary?"

Joe nodded. "Goin' to be a rip-snorter, too, judgin' by the way folks is emptyin' out of Silver. Why, not ten minutes ago the Colonel was over here talkin' about opening up a branch over there if the Chief wasn't figurin' to put a bank in on his own hook. That camp—"

"Where's Frodsham?" Hague said, cutting the eulogy. "I've got to have a talk with him."

The barman waved an airy hand. "Out back, someplace. We're loadin' some of the stuff. Go right on out if you want to—take that door to your right."

"Thanks," Hague grunted, and swung on his heel. But with hand on the knob he paused, struck by a sudden odd quiet in the room behind him. He wheeled a look across his shoulder—and went still. Stopped tense halfway across the room was a man in a cream-colored Stetson. For a moment startled wonder gripped the lines graven in his face; they twisted then beneath some new, more volatile emotion.

" *'Half-a-sec' Hague!*"

They were almost a wail, those hoarse choked words that squeezed past the man's gleaming teeth. The eyes in his livid face were like two bullet holes drilled through an aspen board and a tremor shook the burly shape as, beneath the impact of High Pockets' cold sardonic gaze, he went back a halting pace.

The Red Onion's crowd stood poised like tailors' dummies, their faces blank as so much wax; not even their eyes revealing breath or movement as they stared in glassy fascination at the Tailbone Rafter range boss.

Such was the shocking power of Hague's past name.

"What are you doin' here, Branton?"

The very quietness in which the words were spoken seemed to break the spell. With a shudder Branton pulled himself together. "I ain't here huntin' you," he muttered thickly.

"I reckon not," Hague said. "An' if you're wise you'll take the next horse out."

The contempt in High Pockets' voice cut into Branton like a lash. His jaw snapped shut with a click that carried plainly across this stillness; two glowing spots of color bit through the pallor of his cheeks.

"You go too far, friend Peter!" he snarled, grinding the words out harshly. "I'm not the man to be driven out of any place—you can keep your threats for men that are fool enough to take 'em. I've business—"

"Let me tell you something, Branton," Hague said softly. "I don't give a damn if you stay or go. But if your business has to do with Frodsham, you'd best forget it. This is not a threat. It's a fair an' open warning."

The man's splayed fingers twitched at his sides, but he dared not draw. Something in Hague's eyes said the thing would not be muffed this time, and he believed it.

While he stood there with the cold sweat standing visibly on his forehead, Hague turned back to the door, putting a hand upon its knob.

On a back-bar mirror he could see Jack Branton standing without movement. The puckered scar showed like a brand above the man's dark mottled face. A lust to murder glared from the half-closed eyes—each rigid angle of the burly shape reflected it.

The old, old pattern, Hague thought bitterly, and with rage-thinned lips he opened the door and stepped across its threshold. Only then did he remember the invitation back of Frodsham's acts, the bait extended by a vanished recorder and by the death of Rosalee's brother.

Instead of opening onto a hallway as he'd supposed—a hallway leading to the back—this door opened into a room. A room that was tense with waiting men.

14

THE SPOKED WHEEL

They were ready for him; one quick glance was
proof of this. Organ Smith stood closest with his
upper body bent beside the left-hand wall.
Ballard, Caprosa and another man hovered to the
right with spraddled fists whitely clamped about
the butts of leveled weapons. Frodsham, with a
thin smile curling back his lips, sat back on a desk
with his narrowed eyes aglow with satisfaction.

High Pockets raked a second glance across this
crew morosely. From the start he'd been afraid
that something like this would sooner or later
unfold before him; it was like a scene snatched out
of his past. As in the past he met it, carrying the
battle to these others, focusing all action on the
man who gave the orders.

Before Frodsham could put his taunt to words,
Hague said: "What have you done with Taiban?"
He hammered the words like blows, adding
quickly: "Why ain't he been in his office?"

Startled by the unexpectedness of these questions Frodsham hesitated. He flung a hang out
toward the right. "That's Taiban over—"

"I'm talkin' about the land and claims recorder! Where is he, damn you? Answer!"

Dull color pounded Frodsham's face. He half rose from his chair. But life, Hague knew, depended on quick action. If powder were going to smoke this room, he'd no intention of being at that time where these men's poised stations had caught him.

In three quick strides he crossed to Frodsham's desk, put a clenched fist on it savagely. "Where's the gun you used to kill young Parshall? *Don't lie, Frodsham!* I've seen your sheriff an' sent him hikin' for greener pastures— Don't tempt me, you crawlin' polecat! I'd as lief put a window in your skull as eat!"

He thrust his face within short inches of the gambler's; leaned further forward as, against his will and despite himself, Frodsham's shoulder-blades backed hard against his chair.

Hague's grin was a gleam of teeth. Ballard and those staring others were behind him; but they'd not fire while he stood this near the man who paid their wages. And before they'd any chance to— before Frodsham could collect his scattered wits, Hague stretched a hand across the desk and hauled the gambler over it.

So swift had been his coup, so astoundingly unexpected, he had whirled the shaken Frodsham round in front of him before the fellow's gaping men could realize the thing that was happening. With an arm clamped under the gambler's chin, he held him with the man's own gun jammed hard against his back.

"All right, hombres! Get out there an' line that bunch against the right-hand wall—every man

113

of 'em!" Hague said harshly. "An' you can tell 'em from me, the first swivel-eyed shorthorn touches a gun is goin' to get Mister Frodsham planted!"

Without the faintest feel of triumph, High Pockets watched the sullen crew file out. They were cowed, but for the moment only. They'd not worry over much about Frodsham's safety once they got from under his glance. And, even if they did, to expect that worry to restrain the crowd in the barroom would be asking a mighty lot. Even before he reached the door, a backward look from Ballard showed how edgy the man was getting. And there was a sulky slant to the cheeks of Organ Smith that heralded quick accounting with the man who'd turned him off of the Tailbone Rafter.

Hague scanned his chances and remarked them hardly favorable to continued health. Without leadership the very weight in numbers of that crowd out there would react to his advantage— but they'd *have* leadership. Ballard would be glad to instruct them with a view toward Hague's swift finish. So would Smith. So would the brother of Long Joe Branton. Grandstand stuff was hell-for-breakfast, but there was time when discretion could prove the smartest part of valor —and this was it!

High Pockets felt no shame in hunting a hole to slide through and, inadvertently, such a hole was shown him.

There came a low, soft tapping at a door across the room. With a quiet-snapped word of caution to the gambler, High Pockets propelled him toward it, suggesting that he open it without fuss. Frodsham, lips twisted in a bitter grimace, did so, and Hague found himself confronted by the sheriff's startled features.

"Well! If it ain't our old friend Virtue!" he said sardonically. "Step right in, compadre. This is sure the time for all good men to come to the aid of the party."

Klarson looked from Hague's mocking grin to the sullen scowl of Frodsham. "What the hell's goin' on in there?" he said suspiciously, backing off a pace, his right hand easing hipward. "You all right, Clay?"

"Sure he's all right," Hague drawled gently, and brought to view the gambler's predicament. He said to Frodsham: "Oblige me by removing the Sheriff's pistol. Carefully, brother—*carefully.*"

Under threat of High Pockets' drop, the transaction was completed without undue remonstrance. From the sheriff, that is. But Hague saw by the tremor of Frodsham's arm what the gambler had in mind. Before his intention could be carried out, Hague slashed the barrel of his six-shooter hard against the gambler's head and, with Frodsham crumpling, hurled his body past him through the door, slamming the barrior shut just as boots thumped out a warning from the saloon behind.

"Quick!" he growled at Klarson. "The recorder's office—an' no tricks, mind you, or they'll be your last!"

Two minutes later "We'll never make it!" the sheriff panted through the din that was ripping up the quiet back of them.

"Oh, yes we will," High Pockets assured him

grimly. "They'll not be lookin' for us there. Lead on, my friend, an' don't try no sudden shouting."

By backways and dingy alleys they quartered up the slope; slinking, flitting figures seldom showing themselves, adhering to the thickest shadows; and where infrequent lights shone on them, sauntering casually, wrapped up in their conversation like reunited friends from distant parts.

When the courthouse hove in sight, Klarson muttered: "You'll know, of course, I haven't any key—"

"That's just too bad," Hague said. "I guess you'll have to smash the door."

In the corridor the sheriff brought up defiantly. "This tomfoolery's gone far enough," he snapped. "You've had your fun an'—"

"Not quite all of it," Hague grinned back at him. He patted the brace of weapons in the waistband of his Levis suggestively. "I guess you'll have to smash that door."

They looked at each other.

The sheriff said belligerently: "D'you want to rouse the place? You know what'll happen, don't you—?"

"I know what'll happen to you," High Pockets answered, and his eyes revealed no humor. "You'd better find that key."

The sheriff stared a moment longer. With an oath he dug a bit of metal from his pocket and inserted it in the lock. There was a click and the door swung back, propelled by Klarson's hand.

"We won't need no light," High Pockets mentioned. "I reckon you know this place well enough to find that claims book in the dark."

"Claims book!'"

"Nothin' wrong with your hearin'. I want to file some location notices. Get busy."

Muttering under his breath the sheriff began pawing round. Light from the corridor streaming through the part-closed door showed the shine of sweat upon his face as minutes passed without result. Hague sat on a counter with his long legs dangling and when the sheriff faced him finally it was with an extreme reluctance that was very patent. "The damn thing's gone!" he blurted hoarsely.

"Gone?" Hague inquired very softly.

"You saw me lookin', didn't you? I've hunted all over! The book's not here."

"Don't you find that a little strange?" suggested Hague, very smoothly, very blandly. "What do you suppose has happened to it?"

"Christ's sake!" cried the badgered lawman desperately. "You don't think—"

"I was wondering," Hague cut in, "if perhaps Mister Frodsham could have borrowed it—say, about the time he borrowed Mister Taiban."

Klarson didn't like that tone. He didn't like the substance of High Pockets' words, nor the look of his highboned face. He backed away with twisted, waxen cheeks.

High Pockets' cold voice stopped him. "We're not leaving just quite yet." He regarded the sheriff thoughtfully. "I suppose," he said, "the copies of these notices are usually filed around here someplace, aren't they? Stamped, mebbe, with the date—possibly signed by the one who files them?"

The sheriff's eyes flashed round him with a

117

ratty look. His expression said that if a hole had opened in the floor just then he would have dived at once, not caring where it went, just so it got him away from the Tailbone Rafter foreman's stare.

But no hole opened and High Pockets' stare became even more disturbing. It pushed the shrinking officer behind the counter and over to a row of filing cabinets and reluctantly placed his shaking hands upon a certain drawer and caused him to pull it open.

"You're learning fast," High Pockets approved, and got up off the counter, moving lithely to the sheriff's side. "Just dig around a bit now and see if you can't find some other notices along our boundary."

The sheriff dug and presently handed High Pockets several oblongs of folded paper. High Pockets said, "While I take these over to the light suppose you get busy with your rubber stamp and get these here extension notices stamped and dated," and he handed Klarson the copies Janes had given him.

The papers taken from the drawer were notices of claims allegedly filed on by five hombres High Pockets had no difficulty in guessing to be hirelings of the Silver City chance-game king. The claims themselves were the Copper Girl Extensions, located by the Rafter hands. It took no mental acrobatics to show Hague what kind of move the gambler had decided on. The disappearance of the recorder was designed to keep the Rafter crew from filing. In the meantime these fraudulent notices were on record, and all that was needed to make them good was posession of the claims.

High Pockets eyed the sheriff reflectively. When he looked up, Hague said: "What did you, Brother Frodsham an' Tommy find to talk about last night in Frodsham's office?"

Where Klarson now was standing, the refracted light from the corridor was too indifferent for any clear showing of expression. But the sheriff's suddenly tense posture left little doubt of his reaction to the question. High Pockets said: "You might's well talk. You're not going out of here till you do."

Perhaps it was the Tailbone Rafter foreman's tone that loosened the sheriff's tongue. At any rate, reluctantly and by dint of diverse promptings, the truth was finally out. Klarson put the best face that he could upon the business, concluding with a plea that roped in circumstance. He said: "What the hell else could I do? Clay had come to me with the flat statement that young Tommy owned him money he didn't see much chance of getting; he said that if I'd help, we might be able to scare the kid into ponying across. Kinda dirty trick, I reckon, but nothin' really out-an'-out bad about it. The kid owed Frodsham the money. I never said I'd throw him in jail if he didn't pay—"

"No," remarked High Pockets coldly. "You just let the poor fool *think* you would."

Klarson squirmed. "But damn it," he whined defensively, "can't you realize the bastard's got the high sign on me? I take his orders or—"

"Yeah," Hague said. "It's too damn bad about

119

you!" He looked the man over grimly. "Fella name of Taiban was in Frodsham's office awhile back—wouldn't be the recorder, would he?"

"No-o," Klarson grunted when he could trust himself to speak. "Man you saw was Yuma. Recorder's name is Jake. They're half-brothers. Yuma's ol' woman was a squaw—surly bitch; an' Yuma ain't much better. Bad lot," he added virtuously.

"Well," said High Pockets, getting up, "you better destroy these things." He handed Klarson the location notices the sheriff had taken from the drawer.

Klarson eyed the papers stupidly. "Uh—did you say—?"

"I said tear 'em up. They're frauds."

"But goddlemighty, mister—"

"*Tear 'em up!*"

"Good God, man! If I do that Frodsham'll—"

"I wouldn't be surprised," Hague cut in dryly. "Call in a couple witnesses now—I want 'em to see your signature bein' affixed to these extension notices. As for Frodsham," he added, grinning, "I'd advise you not to be around when he discovers what you been up to."

15

HAGUE READS THE SCRIPTURES

Things had quieted down considerably in the vicinity of the Red Onion by the time High Pockets got back there hunting for his horse. The roan still dozed at the hitchrack and, though its continued presence might well be a trap, High Pockets did not so consider it, figuring that if any of Frodsham's bunch had noticed it, they'd never dream he'd be so foolhardy as to return to it.

He climbed up into the saddle and turned the animal toward the open range. Frodsham's crew might not be expecting him to return for the horse, but that did not mean by a jugful none of Frodsham's men were posted along the trail with rifles awaiting his appearance.

He rode across the range wrapped up in gloomy contemplation of the thing that was before him. He had to break the news to Rosalee of her only brother's death. No pleasant prospect in any sense, he found it doubly difficult considering the manner of Tommy's wind-up and the lad's well-known connections with the boss of Silver City.

He reached the Tailbone Rafter just as the cook

banged the breakfast triangle. He pulled the gear from the weary roan and turned the animal into the big corral, fetching it an armful of hay, then going to the bucket outside the bunkhouse and splashing his face with water. He ran wet fingers through his hair, rasped a thoughtful hand across his chin and concluded he'd do his shaving after grub. The talk with Rosalee could wait till that time also.

Breakfast was a quiet meal. None of the boys did any great amount of talking. One or two asked questions about the mine, which Hague answered with a preoccupied brusqueness not conducive to further queries. As they finished, one by one the men rolled smokes and, rising, sauntered out. Hague kept Roberts with a glance.

"How're things goin'?"

" 'Bout the same as usual," Roberts grinned. "Boys are kinda excited 'bout this copper. Been havin' any trouble with that Silver City bunch?"

"Nothin' worth talkin' about—"

"We heard you'd had a fight with Frodsham," Roberts mentioned. "Any truth in that story about you shootin' Tranch?"

Hague was in no mood for talking of his exploits. He said: "I'm a little worried about the pard of yours, Gene Duncan. You picked him out as one of the five I asked for the other mornin' an' he's out there at the mine. Him an' the other boys have staked out claims below our boundary. Point is, though, Duncan's in a damn bad spot. Smith an' the rest of the Frodsham's crowd'll know it was him put Miss Rosalee onto that copper an' he's right out there in the open any time they want to spot him. I don't like it,

Roberts. Can't you think of somethin' we might mebbe do to get him back here? I'd feel a heap easier in my mind about him—"

"Shucks, don't waste energy frettin' about that guy!" Roberts grunted. "That hombre was weaned on a six-shooter—his ol' man was one of the best all-round pistol shots in this country. Gene's plumb able to take care of hisself."

Before High Pockets could unlimber his cynicism, Roberts added: "Best leave that lad right where he is, Chief. He'd likely take it pretty personal was you t' ship him back here. Expect he'd reckon you didn't figure he measured up."

High Pockets sighed. These bright young lads were all alike: priding themselves on their ability, packing chips on both their shoulders, ready to see it little short of insult were each not chosen to Horatio's envied post. Reflection hinted that he'd once been more than a little partial to such cockeyed notions himself; maybe he *had* been once—but not any more! Show him a man on the Rafter payroll who stood even the remotest chance of filling his boots and that man sure could have 'em. With all High Pockets' blessings!

He sighed again. "Young Parshall's been killed in town. I've got to go break the news to his sister. You can favor me in the meantime by gettin' a fast, endurin' pony under saddle. I've got to hightail it back to camp, an' somethin' tells me it's goin' to be kinda important for me to get there in a hurry."

High Pockets dragged the hat from his head as Rosalee held open the door with a quick, bright smile. "How—?" she began, and stopped, regard-

123

ing him oddly, with the color fading from her cheeks and with her smile gone suddenly twisted. "Pete!" she cried. "What's wrong?"

Hague said: "Well—uh—you see, ma'am . . ." He couldn't meet the searching of her eyes. It was no good telling himself that bluntness, after all, was best. A fellow couldn't barge up to a girl like Rosalee and tell her some damn skunk had sent her brother over the hump. But how else *could* he tell her? What could he find to say that would in any worthwhile measure soften the ugly truth?

Something roused him to the realization she was speaking.

"Sorry, ma'am," he said. "Mind ridin' that trail again?"

"I said look at me! I want to know the truth, Pete. Has something happened to Tommy?"

"He's dead!" High Pockets blurted.

For a second it looked as though she'd fall. She swayed against the doorframe, one hand caught at her breast. A whisper of escaping breath came from her as Hague reached out to steady her.

Her eyes got wide, got dark. She said huskily: "You see now what you've done?"

High Pockets' stare was blank. "*I've* done?" he echoed bewilderedly.

"Yes—*you!*" she cried accusingly. "If you'd let me have my way about that copper, this couldn't have happened. This is Frodsham's work and you're responsible! You said we had to fight him and pitted yourself against him; wickedly, deliberately! All you understand is violence—tumult. There's no diplomacy in you! All you know is fight! fight! fight!" she cried at him bitterly.

"Oh, I *hate* you! Why did you have to come here?"

For a moment High Pockets stared at her, helplessly, abashed.

Then temper had its way with him. "So violence is all I know, eh? Well, it may be you are right ma'am. But I recollect this very plainly: It was *you* said we would fight!"

Her eyes blazed back at him, furious. "Dare you throw it up to me?"

High Pockets laughed—a short, unpleasant sound.

She said: "Get out!" Her voice was choked with anger. "Do you hear?" Her hand rose trembling, pointing down the path. "Get off this ranch and stay off!"

Cheeks white, High Pockets eyed her. He made no move to go, but stood with both scarred fists locked at his sides. It may be he was considering the things she'd said to him; perhaps he was recalling how, earlier, he'd foreseen some such eventuality as this. Possibly he was not thinking at all—just feeling.

But suddenly a cold amusement shone from the eyes with which he met her harsh regard. A cold repression marked his tone. "How long," he said, "d'you reckon you'd last if I did that? How long d'you think you'd *have* any Rafter? Come down to earth, girl! You're old enough to face life's facts. You're living in a hard, tough land; you're up against a hard, tough crowd—the kind that's used to taking what it wants. You've said all I understand is violence. I do understand it—*well.*"

He met her scorn with scorn in kind; said

grimly: "I'll go when my job here's finished," and wheeled away to snatch his reins from the staring Robert's hands.

He got into the saddle stiffly and rode away with his glance straight front.

He reached the copper camp at nine o'clock and found unwelcome news awaiting him. Washout Lunkan, Kettle-Belly's brother, grabbed him urgently by the arm as he swung down from the saddle.

"Thank God you're back," he grumbled fervently. "I ain't seen half this trouble since the big washout that put me outa the cattle business an' made a bean-eatin' nester of me." He took off his glasses and puffed on them, polishing off the steam with a huge, bright red bandana.

"What's up?" Hague asked him sharply.

Washout put his glasses on and squinted. "We better go to the office," he said finally, and led the way. "No sense airin' our troubles in public."

Inside the bare, unfriendly shack, Hague said: "Let's have it."

"Well, in the first place," Washout growled, "a bunch come up from the hollow an' tried t' jump them extensions. Your boys beat 'em off, but in the scrimmage Gene Duncan got his comeuppance an' has since kicked off. Wait—!" he snarled. "That was bad enough. But there's consid'rable worse an' more of it."

He looked at High Pockets keenly. "Them squatters you've taken on kind of look to me fer guidance. Well, I wouldn't do nothin' without your say-so, not knowin' how far you'd want to go. But the truth of the matter is, my friend, there's a tough bunch of monkeys come up from below an' staked out claims on Rafter land—they're all around Discovery."

High Pockets swore. Before he could speak further, a tall, lank man with a stubble of beard on his lean roan cheeks came stamping in.

"Mister Hague," he said, "I dinna ken whether ye're busy or no, but I'd like yer wor-rd on a matter. D'ye stand fer high-gradin'? Or are ye set ag'in it? The lads are draggin' out a powerful sight o' jewelry rock an' sellin' it i' the toon. Will ye stan' fer it, mon, or won't ye?"

"I won't. You tell them birds, McPherson, the first guy caught high-gradin' will get thrown out on his ear. I'm payin' them fellows plenty—I'll not stand for stealin'! If you can't stop it, I'll put a change room in an' strip every shift comin' out!"

With a dour Scots grin, McPherson left.

Hague looked at Washout Lunkan.

"So they've staked out claims on Rafter land. Anyone talked to 'em?"

"Sure, I told 'em they were wastin' their time stakin' any hopes on patents—" He broke off with a scowl. "I'll tell you what I think; I think these squirts have been sicced on by Frodsham. They're not regular copper-stakers. They're *tough*. I think they're *wantin'* trouble! I think they was put in here to *make* trouble—I don't think anythin' short of gunplay'll move 'em."

He looked at Hague consideringly. "I got a hunch this play's intended to bring the sheriff in." His regard was very bright.

Hague scrubbed his eyes with knuckles, took a pace or two about the room; wheeled his shoulders savagely round. "So you think they want trouble, do you?"

Washout said: "I'd take this a little easy, boss. If I got them cougars figured right, they're hopin' you'll get violent. Looks like it might be kinda risky playin' into their hands that way. The sheriff is a Frodsham man—"

"Not no more, he ain't," Hague said, and gave the man a cold, thin smile. "If Klarson's not an absolute fool, he's clean on out of the country."

"Like that, eh?" Washout said, and whistled. "You work pretty fast."

"An' can work a damned sight faster," Hague said bleakly. "Who killed Duncan?"

"A wart named Smith from over in the Organs."

High Pockets ate his cold and considerably delayed breakfast under the ponderosa pines that were dropping welcome dapples of shade across the Copper Girl Extensions. He listened to what the Rafter hands had to say of the claim-jumping expedition from Bonanza, making few remarks and seemingly content to let them outline the incident in whatever fashion best suited them. But when they'd finally done with it, he asked, "About how many fellows were there?"

" 'F you mean how many took part in the fracas," Bill Janes growled, "I'd say six-eight hombres anyway—mebbe more."

"Anyone else got any ideas on the subject?"

Apparently no one had.

"An' Smith was with 'em, eh?"

"Hell's fire!" Janes cried impatiently. "Ain't we told you forty times it was him dropped

128

Duncan? *'Course* he was with 'em! He was *roddin'* 'em!"

"How many of you saw him fire the shot that finished Duncan?" Hague insisted doggedly. Their answers didn't leave much doubt on the score of the ex-Rafter rider's guilt. The looks directed at High Pockets were rather expressive, too; but the strict gravity of Hague's bronzed cheeks remained unchanged.

Breakfast finished, he fished out the makings and left-handedly rolled a smoke. Still with that reticent, inscrutable look upon his high-boned face he took a match from his hatband. He appeared to consider it quite a while before finally striking it on a thumbnail, lighting his quirly and, breaking the match in two, thoughtfully depositing it on a rock. The fragrance of the smoke lazily curling from his nostrils soon exerted its influence on the others and, one by one, they rolled smokes of their own.

They might as well have been in Silver for all the notice Hague took of them. He seemed wrapped up in his thoughts and lounged for a long time with his back against a tree, a far-off look in his squinted eyes, his scarred hand remaining unoccupied at his side. At last, however, with a kind of sigh, he stubbed out the butt of his quirly and pulled the brace of six-guns from the waistband of his Levis.

He spent some moments examining them, shook out their cartridges and replaced them with fresh loads from his pocket. Then, putting the pistols back in his belt, he got abruptly to his feet, the Rafter hands watching him curiously.

He took a long look through the spruce. Quietly

facing the expectant men he said: "Are you gentlemen feelin' the need of exercise?"

They were—to a man.

"Might be a little trouble come up," High Pockets remarked casually. "I'm figurin' to put a few fellows off Rafter land."

The Rafter riders grinned.

High Pockets turned and moved off toward Discovery. Still grinning, the Rafter hands swung in behind.

Hague seemed not to notice McPherson as he strode past the mine office. He did not return the mine boss' nod, but in his lithe and leisurely fashion, kept on going till he brought up at the first of the placed-illegally stakes on Rafter's patented land. Two men had been standing there watching him; as he came up they shifted the rifles in their hands and, with a scowl, the taller of the two growled: "What you huntin' for—trouble?"

"I came over to tell you boys," High Pockets said gravely, "that you've staked out patented land."

"Now ain't that just too bad," the fellow sneered. "You expectin' me to break down an' cry?"

"No," said Hague. "I'm expectin' you to clear out."

The tall man looked at his companion and laughed. The other man laughed a little, too—though without the tall man's confidence. He said placatingly: "We been told this land is free to file—"

"You been told wrong. Might've paid you boys to look up title before going to all this trouble—"

"It wasn't no trouble to us," the tall man jeered. "If there's any trouble about this business—"

"There won't be," Hague said softly. "This is movin' day, boys. Pack up."

The stakers of other illegal claims had drifted up. They made a fan-shaped spread behind the first two. They stood motionless, tense and wary, eying High Pockets with a reticent care, loaded rifles gripped ready in their hands.

Lean and sinewy men these were, one or two displaying the sallow countenance of an indoor man, but the bulk of them showing the bronze of many suns. Picturesque and colorful they seemed in their varied garb, but they were patently neither cowboys nor ordinary miners. They had the look of cold efficiency as they stared across the hush with wooden features.

"Who's boss of you boys?" asked High Pockets suddenly.

The men's eyes flicked to the tall man at their front. The man said, "I am," and spat contemptuously beside High Pockets' boots.

High Pockets said—and there was a strained, hardheld repression in his voice: "Next time you see Clayton Frodsham, you can tell him for me I'm goin' to hold him personally accountable if another of these stunts is pulled. That's all, boys. Pack up an' hit the trail."

The tall man's eyes showed a bright derision. "Pack up yourself if you don't like it. We're here, an' we're here to stay—"

"If you're here when I finish counting to three you'll stay here, certainly," High Pockets said. "One—two—"

The tall man's eyes reflected momentary doubt. He raked a glance at the rifle-toters back of him. Snapping his jaw around he snarled:

"No cocky — — — can tell *me* where t' head in at—"

Like a burst of light Hague was onto him. In a gleaming arc he brought a pistol barrel smashing across the fellow's face, driving him reeling, screaming, backward against the men behind. Without mercy that flashing six-gun struck again. Its impact was a sickening thud, choking off those awful screams, dropping the man loose-jointed, senseless, on the ground.

Hague stood over him, breathing hard, the gun still gripped in his fist. "Come on, you imitation badmen! Make good that brag or hit the trail!"

There were tough men in that outfit, men whose pasts had left their scars for all to see. But something in the bent-torso posture of the hard-shouldered man before them seemed to be exerting a restraining influence, seemed to be turning them from their purpose. Passion's glow faded out of their faces; several shuffled uneasy feet, impatient to be gone. Though some of their number still held notions, resolve was weakening, undermined by the wayward light in Hague's grim stare.

"Well?" he said, and his cold eyes shone maliciously. "What're you wildcats waitin' on?"

The glances of these men turned sullen, shied away from the scornful searching of the range boss' gaze. But his sardonic regard stayed with them, kept on fleering them till the man he'd hammered unconscious rose groaning to an elbow.

Hague said then, "How are you, Jack? Ready to continue that discussion, are you?"

The man crawled stiffly to his feet. His eyes glared mingled fear and hatred, but he kept his hands well away from his body.

"Cut loose of them rifles!" Hague's words were a snapped command.

Fear or a belated caution appeared to have regimented the ranks of these bad-hatters. With scowls they let go their weapons.

"Clear out," Hague told them harshly. "Don't let me catch you inside this wire again."

16

"MONKEY" JANES

After the routing of the copper-stakers, Hague sent the Rafter men back to their claims and turned to find Washout Luncan regarding him peculiarly. The nester boss said reproachfully, "You might of asked my boys to help in that thing."

"Your boys," said High Pocket coldly, "were given a lesson they should profit by. Rafter's payin' them good wages and expects the money to be earned. The next time any Frodsham crowd sets foot this side of the wire, I'll expect them to unlimber prompt an' do their talkin' after."

Washout's glance shifted round a bit under Hague's cold bright regard. But there was iron in Washout's makeup and he said with abrupt defense: "The boys took their cue from me, boss. I told you when you got here why we didn't do no smokin'. We didn't understand your plans an'—"

"You understand 'em now. No man's to cross that wire without my set permission. Warn everyone back; those that won't go throw down on. There are no exceptions, Washout. The only law

134

this country understands is packed on a fellow's hip."

They stared at each other, silent.

A grudging admiration gleamed in the squatter's eyes. "By God, I admire your guts."

Hague scowled at the fellow's compliment. "This is war." His voice was harsh. "Only the hard can survive," he said, and moved like an old man toward the bunkhouse.

It was after seven when he emerged, rubbing sleep from his eyes, and followed his men to the wagon where savory odors from Kettle-Belly's steaming pots put hungry looks about the mouths of the assembling crew.

The sinking sun threw purple shadows across the tawny earth, and a gusty breeze shouldering down from the upslopes, brushed sweating bodies with a welcome coolness.

McPherson, stopping beside Hague a moment, said, "We're drivin' a tunnel. Made forty feet the day an' the vein is widenin'. The lass has a rich thing here, mon."

High Pockets nodded. "Have you stopped that ore stealin?"

McPherson eyed his horny hands. "I've put a wee crimp i' the business. Ye'll ken—"

Hague said curtly: "I want it stopped," and strode away, leaving the Scot looking after him dourly.

Hague was eating his supper when Washout came over with a loaded pan and eased down on the log beside him. "Things've quieted down," he reported. "I guess you've put the fear o' God in them birds below," he said with a grin, and gestured with his fork toward the Frodsham camp in the hollow.

But Hague didn't grin. Without comment, he continued his eating in silence.

The squatter looked at him curiously and, with a shake of the head, attacked his grub. He munched noisily and with evident relish. But he was filled with news and not even Hague's gloomy preoccupation could still his tongue for long.

He said: "Quite a town they've got down there —spread way across the hogback an' halfway up the slope behind. Must be four-five thousan' people, an' more comin' in all the time. Trail's showin' dust clear to Skillet Mesa. We're goin' to put this country on the map!"

"Not many minin' men among 'em yet," he said, "but they'll come all right, don't you worry. Half the town of Silver's here already; they've got shops an' stores an' gamblin' shake-downs an'— Hell, you'd never believe only day before yesterday there wasn't ten people around here! Every hooker in Silver's come, an' Jess Crandle, the queen of 'em all, has got the biggest joint in town! A big cloth place strung on two-by-fours.

"An' Frodsham's here," he added. "His stuff come in in the night. He brought all the carpenters he could get his hands on an' never asked their experience! Got a big place up already —board an' tarpaper. Calls it the Copper Bar an' she's goin' full blast with three shifts of gamblers workin'—"

"You say Frodsham's there himself?" Hague asked.

"Sure! An' his whole crowd's come in with him.

Caprosa, Ballard, Taiban—they're all there! An' some new bird—a stock promoter or somethin'—come in this afternoon from Phoenix; an' Senator Slade's coming down from the Capital. I tell you, we're goin' to make this country hum!" he declared enthusiastically. "There's wagons—Holy Cow! you never seen so many freight wagons in your life! An' tents—they're bringin' in enough fer forty circuses! An' can goods an' the real McCoy in cases! Only drawback to the whole shebang is the distance they got t' pack their water—they got t' go clear to the Sapillo t' get any fit to drink! Fella was tellin' me if you'd let 'em through—"

"Nothing doin'. First one of that crowd I catch this side of the wire is goin' to get what he's askin' for."

Washout said dubiously, "Mebbe they'll get to thinkin' that way about you. That kinda stuff can be carried too far—"

But Hague wasn't listening. He said abruptly: "Did I hear you say some big promoter had come in?"

"Yeah—big talker. Some one-candle power squirt name of Wesley—"

Hague's tin plate rolled to the ground with a clatter as with a sudden oath he caught the squatter boss by the arm. "*What* Wesley? Is his first name Wallabye?"

"Hell—I dunno! For the love of God, leggo my wrist before you break it! You dunno your strength, bucko." Rubbing his aching wrist, he gave a good impression of a slow man trying to think. "Seems like it had a kinda sound like that, but I don't think it was Wallabye. Seems t' me it was more like Willow—Wait! I got it. H. Willoughby Wesley! He's got his name ten inches high on a tent near Frodsham's honkeytonk."

"Is he," Hague asked thinly, "a soft-lookin' mug with tailor-made clothes an' a Stet-hat?"

"Well—" Washout rasped a calloused hand across his jowls, "I dunno's I'd call him soft-looking, but he wears store clothes an' a ten-gallon hat. He's a tall duck—almost as tall as you, I reckon; but thin—hell, he'd have to stand twice t' cast a shadder."

Hague sat hunched and moveless for several long drawn moments. His glance held a far-off, glassy look that took no account of plain-view objects. He was like a man concerned with fragments from his past; but when Washout went back to his eating, he fished the makings from a pocket and mechanically rolled a smoke. Then he sat awhile with squinted gaze in the distance, the unlit quirly hanging forgotten from a lip.

Washout looked at him covertly from time to time and built a few conjectures while shoveling grub to his face. When his plate was empty, he picked up Hague's and took them both to the wagon. "Say," Janes hailed, "I hear you boys been East a time or two—that right?"

Washout chucked a glance at his brother and Kettle-Belly grinned. "I hope to spit in your soup, by cripes!" and the two of them started chuckling. Janes winked at a couple of his friends and the Rafter hands gathered round. "I hear," said Janes, "you fellas can imitate a couple of monkeys at the Zoo. Some of the boys here ain't never seen no monkeys—how about puttin' on your act?"

138

"Well," said Washout, polishing his glasses, "We mostly do it on Sundays, but I expect it can be arranged." He looked at Kettle-Belly. Kettle-Belly nodded. In unison he and Washout stooped and rolled their trousers to the knees. Then they poked their Stet-hats flat like pancakes and placed them canted on their heads. With tongues thrust under their lower lips and sparkling eyes rolled brightly, they began a series of weird perambulations. Kettle-Belly's antics took him close to Janes. With suddenly intent stare he pounced to snatch an imaginary flea from the cowboy's shoulder, appearing to put it in his mouth. Displaying a foolish grin, Washout waddled over and started pawing through Janes' clothing, every so often paused with a pleased expression to thrust something in his mouth. Janes' face got red and the watching cowhands snickered.

Abruptly, with a surprised ejaculation, Kettle-Belly trotted over to a rock and squatted, grunting happily while examining some things he'd got from one of the puncher's pockets. Most of the things he tossed aside at careless random. A bit of lace he carefully spread upon a knee to disclose a lady's kerchief. He sniffed at it and rolled his eyes and the cowboys guffawed mightily and slapped each other on the back while looking from the exhibit to Bill Janes' scarlet face. Then, with lips pursed in a soundless whistle, Kettle-Belly held up a well-worn purse and with a gurgle of delight Washout joined him. They proceeded to open it with exaggerated expressions of hopeful curiosity. Kettle-Belly pulled four crumpled bills from its interior and spread them ostentatiously upon the knee which displayed Janes' sourvenir of romance. Hardly had he done so than with a grunt Washout grabbed up two of them and started waddling off. Dropping purse and kerchief, Kettle-Belly thrust the remaining two in his pocket and took out after him.

Janes' discomfited countenance underwent a change. He yelled indignantly: "Hey! That's carryin' things too far! Come back here with that money!"

The clowning Luncans stopped on a dime. When the scowling Janes came up it was to find himself confronted by a pair of leveled pistols.

"What the hell!"

"My sentiments exactly," Washout growled. "Shove off. You've had your fun. Them as dance must pay the piper. Now clear out of here 'fore I bore you—" The rest was drowned in the hearty guffaws of the watchers. With a sickly grin Janes took off into the timber.

Sun's final glow was gilding the yonder hills with flame when High Pockets rose with a sigh. Discarding the unsmoked cigarette he rubbed the pins and needles from a leg that had gone to sleep, then stood awhile with the half frown of a man considering something that he'd rather put aside. Twilight, where he stood this side of the Gap, was already thickening into dusk, and off across the hollow the campfires of the copper-seekers made bright holes in the swirling gloom.

He was at the corral lifting his saddle from the kak-pole when Washout and Kettle-Belly joined him. "Goin' somewheres?" Kettle-Belly asked;

and when he returned no answer, the cook said, "Fine large night for a ride."

Washout nodded. "We was thinkin' of takin' a little pasear ourselfs," he murmured, and lifting the rope down from his saddle, followed Hague inside the corral.

High Pockets regarded them dourly. "You fellas better stay here. Where I'm goin' there's apt to be trouble—"

"Just what I figured," Washout told him.

And Kettle-Belly, with a chuckle, added: "We're Trouble's little side-kicks—go ask Mister Monkey Janes."

17

UNEXPECTED ENCOUNTER

There'd been no engineers with handy stakes for laying out a townsite when Bonanza mushroomed from the tawny soil, but the stampeders after copper weren't worrying anything about that; they plopped down any place like locusts and the night roared wildly to their din. The locators of claims could give no title to the land, but they'd sell anything they could get their hands on if the sucker showed hard money; and there were plenty of changes involving no cash, occurring through nerve and by force.

The night was bright with campfires and the lanterns and torches of brothels. Dust was thick upon the street and rose in clouds from passing wagons. Intermittent boardwalks, fronting the business places of enterprising merchants, were jammed with jostling people, and the sound of pistol-punctuated oaths and laughter was a constant, vibrant hum.

On every hand board-and-tarpaper shacks were replacing hastily-erected tents, and here and yon log structures rose like forts among their flimsier neighbors. Assayers, promoters, patent-medicine vendors and other capitalists had their wagons and shanties sandwiched in between the larger rig-ups housing games of chance, honkeytonks and bars. Oil flares, placed at appropriate intervals, illumined the crude and misspelled legends daubed across their fronts and painted on the occasional signs that swung from sturdier buildings. Saloons and gambling halls were in the big majority, with brothels and cribs close runner-ups. There were several blacksmith shops, five corrals, eight vendors of general and miscellaneous merchandise carted in by wagon across the baking miles.

The crooked road fairly teemed with life, was reeking with sweat and color. Cow-punchers rubbed elbows with hairy-faced Cousin Jacks; sleek, overdressed bunco-steerers, pimps and cappers walked cheek by jowl with mining engineers and cattle barons. Tinhorns of every description, barkers, claim-jumpers, boomers, desert rats and prospectors with college educations behind them mingled freely and enthusiastically in the flotsam-jetsam composing Bonanza's boisterous population. On every hand one could see the burly shoulder of sunburnt fellows in big hats sauntering and swaggering with the rolling gait of dismounted horsemen. Even more of this gesticulating carefree crowd had hands that were grimed and cracked from grubbing in the soil, cliffs and gullies of the nearby mountains. Whooping riders ripped the dust of the street hat high.

Hague and his two companions racked their horses at the hitchrack fronting the sprawling building whose sign proclaimed it the COPPER BAR. Crude as was the outside of Frodsham's new resort, its interior brought bright sparkles to eyes gone dull and haggard. It was plain that its poker-faced proprietor expected it to bring him in a deal more revenue than the greatest copper lode on record. He'd equipped it with a lavish hand. A mighty copper-colored bar ran lengthwise of the room a full distance of eighty feet and was, when High Pockets and the Luncan boys stepped in, almost hidden behind the shouting press of thirty customers. The gaming tables girdling the orange-painted walls were surrounded by tense throngs. Gamblers officiated with six-shooters prominently displayed; and the place was studded with lookouts on high stools who sat with pistols naked in their laps and hats pulled low across hard eyes that raked the crowd in hopes of finding trouble. Monte tables were piled high with gold and silver, belying the rumor that the camp was short of money. Feverish silence hung over the faro tables and above them extra lamps made glowing blobs through the gathered swirl of tobacco smoke. Off yonder, dealers fresh from supper were putting new games in order, and the snicking click of roulette-wheel balls vied merrily with the shaken dice in chuck-a-luck boxes at stir-ring sluggish blood. Oil paintings hung at inter-vals along the garish walls, and light was re-flected in thousands of sparkles from glass and brass and the gilt on every chair.

Hague swept the scene with a keen, hard glance, giving special heed to the lookouts. There'd be men in here who'd little cause to like him—Caprosa and Ballard undoubtedly, and perhaps some of those fellows who'd tried to stake on Rafter; but if he thought of this, no shadow on his highboned face disclosed it.

There was an eager, kind of wistful light in the eyes of his companions as they keened the crowded tables and looked with longing toward certain silk-gowned dames with mascaraed eyes and alluring smiles who were mingling with the patrons.

"Say!" exclaimed Kettle-Belly, suddenly pointing. "Lookit that, will you? Some class to that baby, eh? Bet she's got more beneath her hair than— Huh? What you pokin' me for?"

"Never mind them hookers," Washout muttered, staring down the room. "Look at the Chief, you nitwit! See where he's headin', don't you?"

Kettle-Belly looked and swore. Hague was headed for a long-geared fellow who, with plenty of company, was sweating a poker game in the room's far corner. The man's back was toward them but they recognized him instantly. It was the black-haired Organ Smith.

Hague had a twenty-pace start and wasn't wasting any time. Washout used his elbows without much care who got them, and those who turned to scowl got shoved aside by Kettle-Belly.

But, half way to his goal, Hague stopped, confronted by a tall slim jack in pin-striped store clothes wearing yellow shoes and a Stetson. "Mister Hague, I believe," this fellow said with extended hand. "I wonder if you remember me? H. Willoughby Wesley is the name, sir. I'm a promoter. I'd like to buy your mine; been hunting all over—"

145

"The Copper Girl," Hague said, "is not for sale."

Wesley looked at his hand, sniffed and thrust it in his pocket. He pulled out a wad of bills—big ones, and waved them under High Pockets' nose. "I'm offering a million dollars!" he said loudly.

"Good Christ!" gasped Washout, staring. "Look what that damn fool's wavin'!"

But High Pockets wasn't having any and he was in no mood to dally. "It's not a matter of price," he said curtly. "The Copper Girl just doesn't happen to be for sale—"

"Two million!" rapped out Wallabye, and shook his gold-knobbled umbrella. "That's more'n I'd intended to pay, but—"

"The mine," Hague said, "is not for sale at any price. Now, if you'll kindly step aside—"

"How about your extensions?" demanded Wallabye doggedly. "I'll give you—"

"The extensions don't belong to Rafter. They belong to the men that located them—"

"But I've talked to the men," the promoter snarled, "an' they all say go to you!"

"Then I'd say it was pretty obvious—"

"Obvious! I guess it is! You may be a great cowman, Hague, but there's a lot of things you'll have to learn. One of them is that you can't deprive all those good-hearted people in the East who've entrusted me with their money—"

Hague grinned at him coldly. "You're wastin' your time an' mine, Mister Wesley. Neither the Copper Girl nor the extensions are for sale. You'll have to hunt up some other bait for the good-hearted people back East."

"That's your final word, is it? Remember—"

Wallabye threatened, "I never ask a man twice!" He looked Hague over shrewdly and a gleam lit the eyes back of his thick-lensed glasses. "You know, of course," he said, lowering his voice, "Clayton Frodsham's after this mine? Well, he aims to get it by hook or crook. A smart man would think twice about going up against a fellow like him. A real intelligent man," he added meaningly, "would grab up an offer like this in a hurry."

"So that's your game, is it?"

"Game? I'm afraid you don't understand the—"

"I understand, all right. You've got three seconds to get out of my path. After that the responsibility's yours."

A wickedness showed in Wallabye's tautened cheeks. "You'll regret—"

"Don't make me laugh," Hague said, and brushed the promoter aside.

Three steps he took and stopped with a jolting abruptness. With dead white cheeks he eyed the startled girl before him.

Young she was, firm breasted, and garbed in a daring, sleazy gown that revealed more than well-turned ankles. But the bold, handsome face was drawn, shocked whiter than High Pockets' own. One hand pressed against her bodice; the other was half extended in a queer, dramatic gesture, as though she wished with all her heart that she could shut him from her sight. Dark eyes, sprung wide, stared intently—alive with incredulity and fear.

She tried to speak. He could see the scarlet lips moving. But no words came.

18

A LIGHT GOES OUT

Well, she'd struck her level, he thought; and
would have passed with a brief civilty had she,
suddenly galvanized to action, not reached forth a
restraining hand. She looked at him wonderingly
—a little hurt her expression said. There was no
cringing in the poised erectness of her body now,
no sign of the degradation advertised by his
finding of her in these surroundings. Gentle
reproach stared out at him from behind the curl of
her lashes.

"Is that all you have to say to me,
Peter-Clyde?" Her husky voice, softly intimate,
ran the favored names together. "After what
we've been to each other?—after all these
months? Is that all you can find in your heart to
say?"

He eyed her grimly. This was that old, remembered voice that once with these low so-tempting
undertones had held such power to sway him—
that had sold him down the river for a string-
pulling sheriff's favor.

"What else?" He grinned derisively. "That

tone an' cooin'-dove look did a heap for me in Texas—remember? I guess I ought to thank you, ma'am; as a teacher you rank high. A little rough, perhaps, but thorough.''

She looked as though another word would break her—would surely send her into tears. With what seemed mighty cost, she got a grip on her emotions; somehow pulled herself together. But High Pockets' glance continued jeering. His knowledge had been costly; she'd not take him in again.

"You're hard,'' she murmured softly; "hard and bitter, Peter-Clyde.'' She leaned toward him and her almost-whispered words held the tinkle of distant church bells. "Have you forgotten so soon the things we told each other? The sacred secrets shared? The tender vows we made together? Our plans for the morrow?''

"No,'' Hague said. "I've not forgotten them any more than you had when you spilled your guts to that sheriff. No, Hettie—I don't reckon I shall ever forget 'em. They were a good lesson, and a warning.''

"Peter-Clyde! You're wrong! You don't realize . . .'' The husky voice held a pleading for understanding; there was almost a sob in it when she said: "It wasn't I who told that sheriff— believe me, Peter-Clyde; it wasn't I—I swear it! I did everything I could to clear you—''

"Even to livin' with the bastard!'' Hague said harshly. "Yes, you were a great help, Hettie. I don't know what I'd've done without you.'' His eyes bit into her, mocked her. "Let's drop the play-actin'. You do it well, but you forget I've seen you in this role before. It's no use, Hettie, we

150

can't go back. Even if I were inclined to believe you, anything you might say is given the lie by this—" He waved a hand at their surroundings, and his glance put the name to her his lips refused to utter.

In that moment she forgot her part, sprang forward and brought the flat of a hand across his cheek with a slashing fury. A ring drew blood as she struck again. Eyes blazing, she backed off with heaving breasts, her face distorted, ugly. Her control snapped utterly by the thing she'd read in his look, she called him every vile name she could lay tongue to; stood trembling, breathing hard, striving to think of some way she could inflict a fitting punishment.

Hague stood eying her bleakly, unconscious of the attention she'd attracted, the hard grin still on his lips. "It does me good to see you actin' natural, Hettie—"

"You cocky fool!" she screamed. "Don't you know that I'm 'Queen Jess' here?—that all I've to do is to give the word and this crowd will tear you to pieces? You can't treat me like dirt under your feet! For two cents I'd—"

"Why don't you, Hettie? It would be in keeping with—"

"God damn your eyes! You'll roast in hell for this!"

"Expect I'm due to roast there anyway," Hague jeered, and sprang past her after a man trying to get through a window.

"It won't wash, Smith. Climb back."

Cheeks grayed by a ghastly pallor, Organ Smith took his leg from the sill. A white-hot craving to get out that window still showed from his frightened eyes; but a dread showed from them also. It was the dread that won. He stood ten feet from Hague's leveled pistol, with shaking knees, and stretched both arms above his head.

It seemed curious to a lot of the watchers that Frodsham's lookouts did not interfere. But the lookouts had good reason for minding their own business. Their pictures were being taken by the gaping muzzles of Washout's and Kettle-Belly's guns.

A deathly hush encompassed the room. Dice and roulette wheels were suddenly stilled; all games broke off, suspended. "Step out of this place and into the street," Hague's quiet voice carried plainly.

It seemed impossible that any three men could do what these proposed. It must have seemed that way to Smith. He stood moveless, eyeing High Pockets sullenly.

Then abruptly, incomprehensibly, amazing even himself, with a half-sobbed groan Organ Smith lurched toward the door. Down a lane that opened wonderingly he moved like a man in a dream.

Hague strode after him to the batwings, faced the crowd with the gun still gripped in his hand till the Lunkan boys had joined him. "You folks better stay where you are," he said, and the three of them followed Smith out.

What they had to do was done quickly; without malice, without excitement. A duty imposed by the times.

Ten minutes later a wild-eyed man burst crazily

152

through the Copper Bar's batwings. "They've hung 'im!" he cried. "They've hung 'im an' gone! I found this pinned to his shirt-front!" He waved a crumpled paper excitedly.

The Copper Bar's patrons dropped everything to rush in, crowding about him—to peer curiously, avidly across the man's shoulders, to read what he had in his hand.

It had the merit of pungency and brevity:

ORGAN SMITH
WHO DIED FOR A MURDER
All
friends and associates
of this man
are
warned to leave the country.

19

JUDGE AND JURY

High Pockets kept his promise to Organ Smith
and wrote the man's mother that night. He spent
a deal of time in the composition of a letter that
would reflect some credit on the dead man's character, discovering several admirable traits to
eulogize which no one had ever guessed Smith
possessed. He wrote reminiscently of the many
high tributes Smith had paid his mother, and the
frequency with which he'd brought her into his
talk. He attributed the roughneck's early demise
to "throat trouble," and signed himself 'Respect-
fully, Peter Clyde Hague, foreman of the Rafter.'

Sealing the envelope and inscribing it to the
lady at the address in St. Louis with which Smith
had supplied him, Hague dispatched Washout to
Silver with instructions to see that the letter got
off on the earliest train.

Washout was back next day at noon with word
that Rosalee wanted to see Hague at the ranch.
"An' damn quick, too, I'd say," he confided,
grinning. "She looked madder'n a broken-backed
rattler!"

154

"What about?"

"You'll hev to ask her. I wasn't feelin' curious."

Hague looked at him, strode across the corral and slapped a saddle on his roan. Ten minutes later he rode through the Gap, leaving Washout's rifle-packing neighbors with plain instructions what to do if Frodsham's crowd hunted trouble.

"What was your idea in hanging Organ Smith?"

Hague stared at Rosalee grimly. "That why you sent for me?"

"Yes!" she threw back at him, blazing. "Why did you do it? What had Organ Smith ever done to you? Can't you do anything but *kill?*"

Hague stood for a moment, silent, scowling down at the clenched fist holding his hat. "I was afraid you'd be takin' it this way," he said quietly. "I'm pretty aware of your hatred of violence, an' I tried to find some other way—"

"You tried!" Her short laugh rasped a bitter sound throughout the room. "I can imagine," she said scornfully, "how you tried!" She lashed at him bitterly: "Your breed can't be happy a moment without spilling blood! How can you stand there holding your head up like an honest man? How can you find the nerve to face me after doing such a thing? If there were any justice—"

"If there were any justice," Hague said harshly, "I wouldn't have *had* to hang Organ Smith—the *law* would have taken care of him! But there ain't no law! You'd not have a man on your payroll if I'd let Smith get away with that! When will you get it through your head that I'm buckin' a bunch of killers? I've got no choice; I've got to fight that gang with *their* weapons! Trigger talk an' rope talk are the only kind they understand!"

"It's the only kind *you* understand!" she stormed. "Violence is all you know! It's your creed! your guide! your pleasure! I'd rather lose this ranch thrice over than keep it at the toll you're taking! I'd rather *give* the copper to Frodsham than see another life lost over it!"

"He's probably countin' on you doin' that. Once let down your guard, or give that man an inch, an'—"

"You're another Bill Bonney!" She cried the name at him fiercely. "You are!" she charged. "*You're just like him!*"

Hague had a hold on his temper. He took the lashing in silence, cheeks stiff, inscrutable, slanted; his hard gray eyes inflinching. When she finished he said, "You haven't asked me yet why I killed him."

"Does it matter?"

"I think it does." Hague's eyes met her eyes straightly. "I helped hang Smith because he deliberately killed Gene Duncan."

"That's a lie!" she told him flatly. "I thought you'd try some line like that. Gene Duncan was killed in a battle—he was killed when that crowd tried to jump the boys' extensions!"

Hague just looked at her. One who knew him would have marveled that he could still control his temper; that little more than a cold repression marked his voice when he said finally, "Your informant's a little careless. Didn't he point out Gene Duncan was the only man killed on either side? He should have; it's signifcant."

156

"What do you mean?"

"I mean that Duncan was killed because he took you out and showed you that copper. Only for Duncan, you might never have known about it —that, at least, would be Frodsham's and Smith's line of reasoning."

"Are you trying," she said, "to make me believe that claim-jumping business just a *blind?*" Her look held little of charity. More indignant than incredulous, it said plainly that he might, with thought, have found some shift less clumsy—some tale sponsored by an appearance of plausibility.

Hague ignored the look.

Doggedly he said: "Smith knew Gene was the one who showed you that ledge; he trailed Gene out there—he's admitted it. That whole raid on Copper Girl Extensions was staged for the prime purpose of giving Smith—an expert rifleman— the chance to snuff Duncan's light."

She tossed her head disdainfully. "Is that your defense for—"

He said coldly: "I'm not making a defense. I'm trying to give you some basis for judging the rights of this matter. Frodsham would never dared have staged that raid for the purpose of jumping those claims—he knows the thing's too risky. I took the trouble to get an official signature on every claim notice filed in Silver. The man who made that signature's missing—which means he's alive. That, in itself, would stop Frodsham from trying any tricks with those claims. It was the Sheriff I had fill in those notices—"

"Then you scared him out of the country so that—"

157

"No; I didn't scare him out," Hague said. "The man's own acts did that." He smiled at her bleakly. "Which brings us back to the core again. The so-called claim-jumping fracas resulted in nothing save Gene Duncan's death. Smith shot him. Smith trailed you an' him to the ledge. What I'd like to know," he said grimly, "is how come Duncan to know about that ore in the first place."

"He overheard Smith and Ballard talking; they discovered it and, rather than have a premature disclosure—rather, that is, than have the news leak out, they invited Gene in, pretending they would give him a share."

She said then without compromise: "What you've told me may be the truth; it seems too far-fetched, too incredible, to be anything else. But whether Smith killed Gene deliberately or not, you had no right proclaiming yourself judge and jury—no right taking the law into your own hands. No explanation you can frame could ever give you that right. If the law in this country's broken down—"

"It's broke down, all right," Hague said. "You hit the nail on the head about that, ma'am. I told you it would at the start."

"Yes." Her glance was a searing indictment. "Then you made your prophecy come true!"

"If you believe that, I guess we've reached the parting of the ways."

Rosalee's voice was not quite even but she had herself in hand. She met his somber glance unflinching. "I think we understand each other."

Hague eyed her for a moment longer. Then with a nod he wheeled and left.

She heard his spurs rasp the length of the hall—
choke off when he left the veranda. Leather creak
told of his mounting.

When the sound of his horse ceased in distance,
she still listened. There were tears on her cheeks
when she turned.

20

SOLD

Hague evidenced no great hurry to depart.

He reached the mine at dusk. Most of the boys still were hanging round the wagon, smoking after liberal helpings of Kettle-Belly's grub. Kettle-Belly himself was in process of cleaning up, but stopped when he saw Hague riding in. "Heve you et yet, Chief?" he hailed.

"Sure," lied Hague, and beckoned Washout aside. "How come your men are not posted?"

"Not posted? The hell they ain't!" scowled Washout, raking a glance round through the gloom. "By God, I put three of them squirts on picket an'—"

"They're not on picket now. You better tighten down on them boys, Washout, or the rest of you'll lose your shirts. Throw this bronc in the corral an' have somebody slap my gear on a fresh one."

Looking after him curiously, Washout scratched his head as he watched Hague enter the office. There was something odd about the Chief's actions, Washout's expression seemed to say. When Hague returned minutes later, Washout said, handing over the reins: "You had a visitor here this evenin'."

"Where is he?"

"Wasn't a he. Queen Jess it was. She's gone."

"What'd she want?" asked High Pockets, scowling.

"Didn't say. But I reckon she was huntin' you. Said to tell you she'd like to see you at her place when you got back."

Hague said nothing, but climbed into his saddle and rode out through the Gap. Washout, polishing his glasses, stood looking after him, shaking his head. "Don't noways pay t' cross a woman that way," he muttered worriedly. "He's sure gone off his feed. Wisht I knew what ailed him."

Three days passed without action, the Frodsham crowd lying low. Rosalee sent no one from headquarters to take over Hague's supposedly relinquished duties. Nor did Hague appear to give much thought to them either. He spent most of his time in Bonanza, sometimes gambling, but mostly sitting at some back table, morose, bleak of eye—like a warning. There were those who believed him hanging round to make sure Organ's friends took the hint; but there were others, more in the know, too aware that the rumor was false, for most of Smith's friends had departed. These men, a select few close to Frodsham, put a darker interpretation to Hague's continued presence and walked with a foreign care. They were extremely polite and left him alone, though his stare was a blight on their business.

Washout was badly worried. He could not understand this change in the Chief. In these

161

days following his return from the brief visit to headquarters, he seemed to have retired within himself—to have become a different man, almost. Things got done, but High Pockets showed no interest in them; he appeared totally indifferent to what Washout believed to be his duties. Something certainly had come over him, and Washout secretly blamed it on Queen Jess. He knew well enough Hague hadn't visited her; but that might mean anything or nothing. The squatter boss felt she was back of Hague's strange preoccupation, and cursed her for it bitterly.

Even McPherson noticed the change. He saw the Chief but seldom, and upon those few occasions that he brought the man reports, he got small change for his trouble. The man offered no suggestions; received good news and bad with silence. It was uncanny, McPherson thought.

To some extent every jack on the mine-crew payroll felt the influence of Hague's sudden change. His jokes were gone; he was curt and caustically saturnine. His glance took on a colder inscrutability, his mouth a more grimly sardonic twist.

The second afternoon after Hague's return from the ranch, a ranger dropped by. For a while he chatted amiably with Washout concerning progress, both of the mine and of Bonanza. Then he said abruptly: "What's come over your boss? Looks like he's soured on the world." Washout shrugged and changed the subject.

When he wasn't sitting dour and hard of eye in Frodsham's Copper Bar, Hague walked Bonanza's dusty streets, his tough face warped to a taciturn slanting. He seldom spoke to folks even when hailed, but on the third afternoon Wallaby Wesley came running up and caught him by the arm. "How about selling me a few sacks of ore, Mister Hague? I hear you're taking out plenty. I'd like to have a little stuff to put on display. I got an office now, you know—regular frame building, painted red, and—"

"No soap," Hague grunted, and would have passed on, but Wallabye tightened his hold.

"I'll label it right," he said. "Where's the harm? You've got to pack the stuff to the railroad before it can be shipped to the smelter. That'll take money, and it's risky with all the hard characters that have started overrunnin' the country. Look—I'll pay you twice what the smelter crowd'll give you an' take delivery right up at the mine. What's fairer than that? Be a crime to pound up ore like that—"

"Nothing doin'," repeated Hague, scowling.

"Not for *any* price?" Wallabye wheedled.

"Not for a million!" Hague looked the man square in the eye.

"How about two million?" Wesley smiled. He thrust a hand into his pocket. "After all, there's a lot of high-gradin' going on, you know. I *could* buy that stuff—"

"Don't let me catch you at it," Hague said, and strode off leaving Wallabye gaping.

He understood well enough the promoter's reason for wanting that ore. Wesley intended to display it all right—but not around Bonanza. What Wallabye wanted was ore to send with fake stock to the East. Ore for the suckers to gaze at; to make them dig open their wallets.

163

He was passing Jess Crandle's sporting house when the woman gave him a hail from the door. Hague scowled and kept on going, but she ran after him as Wesley had, catching a hold on his arm.

Without rude force he could not disengage her. Having no wish to attract undue attention he stopped and turned, looking down at her grimly. "What is it?" he said curtly.

He found her regarding him searchingly; her dark eyes, strangely sober, holding a wistfulness —a mute appeal that could have moved him once. She stood with her lips a little parted; well-shaped they were, full, ripe, and of a crushed-berry redness. But they had no power to move him now. He stared back at her unblinking.

"Forgive me for what I said the other night—I was angry, out of sorts, hysterical. Try to believe in me, Peter-Clyde," her pronouncement of his name was a soft caress. "I told you the truth about the past. I *did* try to help you, and you're wrong when you say I lived with Carrolton—I never did that—I *couldn't* have. Can't you realize—?"

"Yes," Hague said bluntly, "I can realize what you're up to, all right. But it won't work, Hettie— you shot your bolt at the Alamo. Your blandishments have lost their charm."

He felt her wince, but she didn't let go of his arm. "You mean—you mean because of this, I'm not good enough for you now?" She waved her free hand at the brothel, her dark eyes searching his gravely. "I'm not a part of that, Peter-Clyde. Oh, I own it—yes. But when you disappeared that night I had to do something. I came to Silver. After all, a girl has to live."

She stared down at her ring, her breathing deepened, disturbing the set of her low-cut gown; her pointed breasts making two sharp cones in its fabric.

He stood rigid, lips tight, saying nothing.

Her shoulders swayed from their droop, the thick gloss of her hair making a halo round her face; the arrangement of it giving added piquancy to features that in themselves were blood-stirring enough. She said softly: "Is that it, Peter-Clyde? Is that why you'll have nothing to do with me?"

Impatience tugged his shoulders. "Your profession's got no part in it. I told you why we're through. You had your chance an' you chucked it. You got sold on the shine of a stare. You used me—But let it go!" he said harshly. "I'll not be tripped that way again."

"You're wrong, Peter-Clyde—I swear it!" She cried rebelliously: "Someone's lied to you if they—"

"I've no doubt of it," he cut in drily. "I choked the truth from Carrolton that night before I left."

"The bastard lied!"

Hague shook his head. "You'll not make a fool of me again."

Her hand fell from his arm, but she faced him bravely. Her red lips made a long and wistful curve against the alabaster pallor of her face. "I guess it's goodbye then, Peter-Clyde. You mean this to be the end?"

"The end is past." He regarded her coldly. "Whatever there was between us, Hettie, is finished. You made your bed that night at Alamo when you tipped Carrolton off to where I was."

He was starting to turn away when her arms closed about him hungrily. "You'll not go without a kiss? Just one, Peter-Clyde—just one for the sake of what might have been?"

The sob in her voice checked his turning. Her white arms locked round his neck, bending his stubborn head downward, bringing his face to her own.

He was reaching, embarrassed, to break her hold when his glance was snapped round by a shadow. Rosalee was passing with Frodsham; a tight smile curved the gambler's lips. His voice reached High Pockets clearly. "Sorry, Miss Parshall, you have to be subjected to a thing like this," he said suavely. "The affair's deplorable. She's told the fellow often enough—but some men can't leave her kind alone. She runs a house of ill fame across the road . . ."

Rosalee turned away white-cheeked. Jess Crandle stepped back with a grin.

Hague glanced at her bleakly and turned to stare after Rosalee. She was hurrying up the street with Frodsham.

With a short, harsh laugh, Hague strode off to find his horse.

21

"SLIPPRIER'N SLOBBERS"

Hague rode south, little caring where his pony took him just so that it was out of the Black Range country, away from Silver City and all of Frodsham's works. The gambler had been too slick for him—he could see that now. He had thought he had the fellow licked, checkmated at every turn; but all the time Frodsham had only been playing possum, toying him along like a cat with a rat until, of a sudden, he'd pounced.

No doubt it was just as well. He was no fit man for a girl like Rosalee anyway; it would be hell for her to fall in love with him. He was a gun man—notorious; hunted by a lesser breed who would gain fame by plowing him under. It hurt to consider what she must think of him after that street scene, after listening to Frodsham's calculated pleasantries. It hurt bitterly, and time and distance were not proving efficacious as he'd hoped.

There'd been a moment that day—one white-hot second as he'd stood there watching Rosalee hurrying off with the gambler—when he'd very near killed Clayton Frodsham, so driving had been the quick-flaring rage that had gripped him.

He took little credit for arresting the impulse; it was foresight had pulled him up, stopped him. Thought of what wagging tongues would have done to Rosalee afterwards.

But she'd named him right—said *violence* was all he knew. That had come pretty close to the truth. It was all he had known these last three years; all he'd known since dropping Joe Branton.

Denying the hunger in his soul, he called himself a fool and drove deeply—ever more deeply south.

He crossed the Border into Arizona; a somber, leather-faced rider whom nobody cared to arouse. A man with two pistols tucked into his jeans and the look of pure hell in his eyes.

Douglas knew him briefly. Agua Prieta, too.

Bisbee knew him, and Tombstone.

In Tucson he lingered longer. He was spoiling for a fight, they thought, and packed him one for the hell of it. Two were still regretting it when he left; a third—the sheriff—was past all caring.

He drifted south again to Tombstone. He was a familiar figure for awhile at the Oriental and at the lusty Last Chance saloon. He entertained the town's sirens in the Crystal Palace and the Alhambra, and saw one or two of the "stupendous attractions" at the Bird Cage.

But he soon tired of the Earps' recent stamping ground. He saddled up his horse one night and rode across to Gleeson, a town just south of Brown's Peak. But there was nothing for him there and the wanderlust was on him. Something was tugging him east . . .

Gaunt, taciturn, hard eyes alert and narrow, he rode one day into Shakespeare, a mining town over in the Pyramids. A collection of one and two-story adobes each side of horse-tracked dust, Shakespeare was not big. But it was tough—plenty. They'd strung Russian Bill and Sandy King—a couple of Curly Bill's long-riders—to a rafter in the dining room of the Pioneer House awhile back; and were not averse to doing the same for other wild sprouts should they chance to outrage the vigilance committee's ideas of the fitting and proper.

Tight-mouthed, dusty and saddle-drawn, High Pockets booked a room at this friendly hostelry and put his horse in the public corral. The room was little more than a pigeon's hole under the sloping eaves, but Hague said nothing and was shortly taken to admire the rafter from which the two outlaws had swung. "An' right at supper time, too, by grab," declared the garrulous landlord. "Had everything on the stove, hot an' set to serve. But d'ye think them consarned stranglers would wait? No, by grab! They says: 'We got important business to hand,' an' shoves back my table free as you please. The grub got dang nigh burnt afore they cut them scalawags down!"

Hague was subject to covert stares and there was considerable speculation. But no one got up sufficient nerve to ask his business. He spent his time in the town's saloons, talked mining sometimes with the hard-rock boys, but otherwise kept to himself.

It was here one night that Washout found him.

Hague said nothing till he and the Rafter's squatter boss were seated in the comparative privacy of the former's room at the Pioneer House. Then he eyed the burly man grimly. "Has—did anyone send you huntin' me?"

"Hell, no!" muttered Washout, staring. "What give you that idear? I shot one of Branton's greasers an' had t' cut my stick."

"Branton?"

"Yeah. I guess he come after your time. He's give out his mine's in copper an' hired him a bunch of Mex'cans to work it. 'F you ask me, though, all he's got's a hole in the ground. He's hirin' them greasers for color. Calls the place the Lucky Bug Lode; he's been tryin' to unload it on the G.O.S.—Charlie give me the job of scoutin' it."

"Aren't you workin' for the Rafter?"

Washout grinned. "Not any more, I ain't." He looked at Hague kind of brightly. "You could've knocked me over with a cedar post when I found you'd got your walkin' papers! I never got wise till a couple days after you'd left. Miss Rosalee come stormin' in one mornin' an' laid the whole crew of us off—"

"She closed the mine?" asked Hague, astonished.

"Naw. Mine's still runnin'—but she laid off all of us guards. Said it was only askin' fer trouble to keep armed guards posted round the place. She sent us packin' quick— Oh, she was fair enough, I reckon. Said any of us as wanted to could have ridin' jobs at the ranch. But, hell! I could see the

170

good ol' days was gone. Me an' Kettle-Belly an' two-three o' the other boys quit. Then along come Charlie an' offered me a hundred bucks to find out if the Lucky Bug was really in ore."

"Was it?"

"I didn't learn. Bunch of Branton's greasers caught me foolin' around the hole one night an' I had t' git out in a hurry. I salivated one of 'em before I thought. Nothin' for it then but run—"

"For pottin' a Mex?" Hague looked surprised. "Self-defense, wasn't it?"

"Well," said Washout dubiously, "that's what we *used* to call it. But, you see,"—he looked at High Pockets slanchways, "Frodsham's been appointed sheriff t' fill out Klarson's term. Senator Slade saw to it personal; he talked the commissioners over."

He shrugged and sighed lugubriously. "The ol' days is gone, I reckon." He said reflectively, "Bonanza's a up-an'-comin' town right now, boy —or it would be if the soap-boxers would leave it alone. Labor's comin' into its own, looks like— stumpers on every corner. Well, what I was gonna say is, this Branton's the new town marshal. Him an' Frodsham is thicker than thieves. An' that promoter guy, Wesley—them three's workin' hand an' glove. Makin' money like the Denver mint. Wallabye got out a slew of fake stock an' took a passel of suckers fer a cleanin'. You never heard of such buyin' in your life! Made s' much money him an' Frodsham's opened up a bank together—the Bonanza Silver Trust. Worth millions! Bunch of Eastern capitalists come in an' bought every claim in sight!'"

Hague said: "What about this Lucky Bug hole

171

of Branton's? Did he think Charlie'd buy it sight unseen?"

"No. He showed it to Charlie three-four times— took him right on down the shaft. But, hell, Charlie don't know nothin' about copper mines; he knows good ore when he sees it; that's all, an' Branton has plenty of that. Stuff looks," he said with a wink, "like the ore them high-graders been liftin' from Rafter."

Hague scowled. "What's the matter with Mac? Can't he stop it?"

"He ain't," Washout said with a chuckle. "I guess he knows which side his bread's buttered on. Frodsham's the brass-collar dog around them parts, an' since Miss Rosalee fired all the guards, what Frodsham says pretty near goes."

Hague took a savage turn about the room.

Washout said: "Sure makes me boil to see the reamin' them damn crooks are givin' her! Give 'em a couple more weeks an' they'll have her froze plumb out entire. She's made Roberts boss of the diggin's an' has give Bill Janes his ranch job. Roberts is all right; he's a good kid, but he can't stand up t' Frodsham. He ain't got the right kinda savvy."

"What about Janes' claim?"

"Sold. Sold out t' some guys in Nevada I heard. Frodsham's runnin' it now. Runnin' all them extensions, far as that goes—him an' Wallabye Wesley. Be runnin' the Copper Girl, too, pretty quick."

Hague caught him by the shoulder. "What's that?"

"Ouch! Leggo! Dang it, bucko, you dunno your strength—get your paw off'n my—"

"What do you mean?" Hague growled, stepping back. "How will Frodsham be runnin' the Copper Girl? Miss Rosalee hasn't sold out?"

"Well, no. She ain't sold out—but she's gonna be." He glared down at his gnarled hands for a moment, then lifted his glance to Hague's face. "You see this Wallabye squirt's talkin' pardners. He says—an' far as that goes it's the truth—he says it takes real money to develop a mine like the Copper Girl; he says it ain't turnin' out a quarter what it could. There's water gettin' into it. He claims it needs pumps an' big minin' machinery. He—"

"Rafter's got money," Hague grunted. "Why'n Tophet don't Rosalee spend a little an' get the kind of machinery it needs?"

"Well, you see," Washout said, "that mine ain't brought her a thin nickel so far. They're runnin' a stage to El Paso now, but a stage can't carry the ore. Roberts has been shippin' that out in freight wagons. Up to date not one of 'em's landed. They leave Bonanza all right, but none of 'em gets to El Paso."

Hague stared. "What about the drivers—the guards? What do they say about it?"

"That's just the trouble. Roberts don't never see 'em again. They go out with the ore an' that's the end of 'em. Last time he put on three guards from Rafter. But they didn't get back from it, neither."

"What happened to them?"

"He ain't found out."

"You mean to tell me," Hague said gruffly, "that all them wagons an' drivers an' guards just disappear—just go out in the desert an' vanish?"

"They don't exactly vanish, I reckon. They go some place, all right. But they don't come back to Bonanza."

"What about El Paso?" Hague asked abruptly. "What do the smelter people say?"

Lunkan spread his hands out. "They claim the wagons don't get there."

Hague swung round; paced the floor in a savage silence. "Bet I'd put a stop to that!" He growled softly: "Go on—tell me the rest of this Wallabye business."

"Well, he says for a half interest in the Copper Girl he'll supply the capital for installin' the proper pumps an' machinery; that he'll open the mine up wide an' put every idle guy in the camp to work. That's brought a lot of pressure to bear; with the whole town workin', that'll throw all these labor agitators outa stride an' the camp'll be rid of 'em. Makes it kinda look like Rosalee's a wrench in the wheels of industry—see? Like the only decent thing for her to do is to let Wallabye in on the deal an' pass out good times for all."

"What's he propose to do about the disappearin' wagons?"

"He claims if any more ore gets sidetracked, she can take it out of his share of the profits."

The two men eyed each other somberly.

"Like that, eh?"

Washout nodded. "Makes a fella think a little, don't it? But," he added reflectively, "he *may* not know a thing about that end of it. Tell you the truth, I don't believe he does. There's a nice fat joker in the deal, all right, but if I got that pelican sized up right, his angle's somethin' else again."

Hague looked at him, waiting.

Washout said: "This Wallabye's a promoter. He's been floodin' the country with stock—ain't been any of it worth the bother of burnin'. But he's sold it—*sold every scrap he could print!* If Miss Rosalee gives him a half interest, what's to prevent him gettin' out stock on the Copper Girl? They all know the mine's got the ore."

"Stock won't necessarily hurt it," Hague began, but Washout cut him off.

"Stock wouldn't, mebbe, some ways," he growled. "But you don't know that Wallabye bird like I do! I've seen what he can do! I've seen the way he works—he's crooked as a dog's hind laig!"

Hague said irritably: "I wouldn't want to see this Wesley in pardners with Miss Rosalee any more'n you would. But on a fifty-fifty proposition, what could the fellow do? If he issues stock he's got to get her consent before he can do it, and—"

"What does *she* know about this stock game? She's a babe in the woods when it comes to dealin' with sharks like Wallabye an' Frodsham!" Washout snarled. "Look where they've got her now! I think I can see what he's up to."

"What?"

Washout puffed on his glasses, wiped them carefully with his bandana, and put them back on his face. "Well, I'll tell you. He played this kinda game on Jim Thompson—you know, Jim had one of them extensions. Wallabye an' him went in pardners, Wallabye put up the cash. It was the same kind of fifty-fifty deal, only Wallabye—after they'd agreed to stock it—declared he ought to have fifty-one percent of the stock to pay for the cost of printin' an' what not. Jim says O.K., that was fair enough. Well, it wound up by each of 'em donatin' twenty percent of their stock for marketin', with Wallabye to have charge of the sales."

He grinned at High Pockets sourly. "The upshot was Wallabye bought in the market stock himself an' threw Thompson out on his ear."

"But Thompson still had thirty percent of his half—"

"You talk that over with Thompson. He ain't been inside the mine since." He looked at Hague significantly, fetched a plug of chewing from a pocket and bit off a man-size hunk. " 'Course," he said, masticating noisily, "he mightn't try anything so raw with Rosalee, but you got to remember that Clay Frodsham's the sheriff an' them two is slipprier'n slobbers."

22

A MAN GETS INTO HIS SADDLE

High Pockets stood a bit, as though considering; the lamplight pulling the contour of his features into sharpened lines and deep, banked shadows. He seemed to be weighing the squatter's words, and as he stood there his cheeks took on a turbulent slanting.

Washout's pulse beat faster and a kind of hope showed in his glance as he thought of just how much this fellow's help could mean to the girl and Rafter. No one had to tell him Frodsham was about to pull his biggest coup. That day Hague had given him a beating he had threatened to break the ranch, and now he was set to do it.

Movement pulled his glance around. Hague was pacing the floor. Each muscled bulge of the fellow's figure showed the power of the man. High Pockets Hague was a name Clay Frodsham had learned to respect. Washout grinned a little. He would not be in Frodsham's boots just now for a million dollars. When this fellow got through with him, Frodsham might not be in those boots, either!

It was a pleasant thought. But brief.

Hague stopped pacing suddenly and wheeled his shoulders square around. "It won't wash, Lunkan."

"Huh?" Washout screwed his eyes up puzzledly. "Talk English, fella. What won't?"

"My goin' back to Bonanza," Hague said harshly. "I can't do it, Lunkan."

Washout's jaw fell open. He stared at High Pockets without belief. "You mean—" he gasped; "you mean you're not goin' back to help her?"

"No."

"Why—hell, man! That 'crowd'll smash her flatter than a last year's leaf!"

"I can't help it. She wouldn't welcome my help, Washout. If she'd wanted me, she'd have sent for me. She told me plain enough that day at the ranch what she thought of me and my services. She as much as told me her brother's death lay at my door. No," he said, mouth twisted, bitter, "she'd welcome no help of mine."

Washout stared at him, astounded. It was some moments before he remembered to shut his jaw. He moved slowly to the window, stared morosely into the night, trying to realize what this meant, striving to encompass the magnitude of this catastrophe, its results to Rosalee and the ranch.

He stood a long time there, unseeing; his shoulders queerly hunched, big fists hanging open at his sides.

He turned at last, not looking toward High Pockets, tramping heavily toward the door. His hand was upon the knob when a whisper of escaping breath from High Pockets turned him. Hague

said: "I'm just a goddamn fool, I guess, but—
Get my roan from the corral for me, will you,
while I settle up my bill?"

23

A LOAN FROM A LAWYER

More and increasingly more of late, Rosalee
found the turning of her thoughts reaching out to
that tough outlander who, for the space of a few
brief days, had been the Rafter's range boss. She
did not like him, *had* not liked him and *never
could* like him; of that much she was certain. But
there was no denying that the man had been
efficient. Rafter had fitted him and he had fitted
Rafter. Not only that, but in some queer fashion
she had never stopped to analyze, he'd been a
comfort to have around. He made you feel that
the world was running smoothly, that it was a
good place after all and that unpleasant things
could not touch you—yet, how many unpleasant
things had!

He'd been a figure of power and influence in
this Black Range country during those gone, fast-
fleeting days. She'd at that time attributed this
to his foremanship of Rafter; now she was not so
sure. Certain it was that Ballard had not wielded
it, nor could young Roberts. Hague had com-
manded a respect; men had listened to his words

and such as had not heeded had been speedily shown the error of their ways. Men had seen in him a dread, implacable fury and had grown to practice a foreign care, fearful lest their acts, discovered, call down grim retribution.

Hague had not been sleek nor smooth. He had not been suave. He'd shown tough and hard and cynical; exasperating, unmanageable. His had been a fighter's bluntness; Rosalee could not be sure she'd rightly hated this—whether, after all, she had not cherished it, been secretly, been foolishly admiring of it.

Though she had not cared for his looks his features had been good enough after their fashion. Strange how well she could recall them; the high flat cheekbones, the stubborn jaw, the clean-shaved, hard, square chin. His hair was of a sandy shade; she recalled the way it tumbled across his forehead in damp, unruly curls. She remembered, too, the tranquil confidence of his glance; its cool and grave directness that had been such irritation, especially at those times she'd been accusing him of violence.

But the mark of the bravo was on him. It was in the angles of that tough and rugged face, in the hardness of pale eyes, in the cynical lines about them, in the sardonic twist of his mouth.

No, she had not liked the man; she *could* not. It was peculiarly exasperating that her thoughts could go so often to him—that she could find some measure of reassurance, some vague sort of peace and comfort in just thinking about the fellow.

His bronzed features were etched as sharply in her mind as though he sat before her; she could almost *feel* him in the room with her, his personality was so strong. Sometimes, like now, thinking of him in this odd, detached sort of way she seemed to sense behind the fire and pride of the man an edge of wistfulness; a remote and carefully concealed longing for something better than he knew. Almost, thinking that way, she was tempted to revise her estimate of him.

Hard, tumultuous, sardonic, she had thought him, and those things he surely was. But was there, back of this paraded toughness, some finer, hidden thing? She recalled now what he'd told her once about himself and turbulence. Had he told the truth? Did he really hate it as he'd claimed that day? Had he really been trying to escape it in coming to this back country?

She recalled their far discussion of the Rafter's new-found copper; remembering how he'd pointed out what would happen if she made up her mind to mine it—how he'd said the choice was hers and she had told him that she'd fight. Could she, after all, have all this time been unwittingly wronging him? The thought made her somehow feel more friendly toward the memory of the man. When one looked at the facts, it was *her* battle he'd been fighting—hers and Rafter's.

Then she recalled the day with Frodsham when, on the main street of Bonanza, she had seen Hague pawing over that creature from the brothel; and all the warmth went out of her. How could a man who would do a thing like that have any good in him? No! High Pockets was lost to shame—lost utterly!

She looked at the man across the table from

her, carefully. Could she trust him? Could she place confidence in the value of his words? Could she feel that what he told her was the truth?

She knew so little of these matters. They were things beyond her experience, beyond her ability to judge. She knew Bonanza expected her to do what he was asking; to give this man half interest in the mine. Such an act would mean salvation, she had heard, for all the idle men in camp, left jobless by the sudden closing down of Copper Girl Extensions. She'd asked many persons in whose judgment she placed confidence, why this man and Frodsham, who controlled them, had seen fit to suspend their operations; and the answers all had been the same—"No ore; the vein's pinched out."

To her this seemed incredible, especially in the case of Thompson's claim which had shown up well. But she supposed her informants knew, a number of them were veteran miners; some had even been engaged in extracting ore from those very holes—who could know better than they?

She said hesitantly, "Would you explain the terms of this contract to me just once more, Mr. Wesley? I'm really not at all familiar with these things, and figures confuse me. Just tell me plainly what this agreement would entail."

"It's very simple," Wallabye said with a quick, hard glance at Roberts. "In exchange for a half-interest in the Copper Girl, I've agreed to furnish, in any amount, whatever capital's necessary to the purchase of new machinery, installation of pumps and so forth, that will ensure, in so far as is humanly possible, proper operation of the mine —consistent, of course, with output. The Copper

183

Girl," he said impressively, "should be capable of three times its present output. The mine is rich, the ore is there, and the only reason it has not been making you returns is the present lack of proper facilities.

"That is so, isn't it, Mr. Kendall?"

The blandly pompous lawyer nodded. "Quite correct, Mr. Wesley; quite correct."

Wallabye turned to the Rafter's foreman. "You've examined the contract, Mr. Roberts. Have you found anything the least bit vague or unfamiliar about it? Anything you found it hard to understand, or that appeared to you out of the ordinary?"

The badgered Roberts, unaccustomed to the contract's legal jargon as was Rosalee, but loath to admit such seeming ignorance, scowled a little and shook his head. "No-o. It looks all right to me. Just that point about the fifty-one percent is all—" He flushed under the lawyer's slightly pitying regard. "I mean, in a straight-out fifty-fifty deal—"

"But I thought Mr. Kendall explained all that," growled Wallabye, with a glance like the draft from an icebox. He said impatiently, "Tell him again, will you, Kendall?"

Mr. Kendall remarked suavely: "There's really nothing unusual in the clause. As originally drawwn up, this contract represented an even sharing of the mine. Upon due examination of the property, however, I discovered that, as Miss Parshall freely admits, past cost of operations greatly outbalanced the sumtotal intrinsic value of all ore mined to date. Furthermore, in consideration of the fact that no moneys at all have yet

184

accrued to the present owner as a result of this mined ore, it seemed only just to me to advise my client, Mr. Wesley, to protect himself by the addition of this clause. A one percent advantage, in consideration of this established fact—and in consideration of the cost of stock printing which my client agrees to stand, is not at all to be construed out of the commonplace in such negotiations, Mr. Roberts, I assure you."

"Far as that goes," Wallabye said magnanimously, "if that's all that's troubling you, I'll waive the matter entirely. We'll have Mr. Kendall strike it out." And he smiled at Rosalee beneficiently.

"No," she said; "leave it in there. I'll not quibble over trifles. If Mr. Kendall feels that you should have that little margin, Mr. Wesley, you shall have it. I don't wish to take unfair advantage."

"I am certain of it," Wallabye bowed.

"Very well," said Lawyer Kendall briskly. "If you'll sign right here, ma'am—" He handed her his uncapped fountain pen. "Yes—that's it; right down there."

Rosalee looked at the paper, but the print was all blurred, run together. Not really, of course; it was just that her mind was so hodge-podge. She couldn't think clearly. All this talk was confusing; Mr. Kendall's words so much Greek. She hadn't thought there could be all this print just to a pardner's agreement. All these "parties of the first parts" and "herein as beforesaids" were just so much gibberish to her.

She wished High Pockets were here to advise her—he would know what to do, she was sure.

24

LAST WARNING

There were crowds of hungry miners on the streets when Washout and High Pockets, three days later, came riding into town. Bonanza was full of agitators flinging brimstone freely, using God and Hell and capitalists in the same liquor-laden breath. There were soap-boxes on every corner, and the stumpers were cursing Rafter; shouting, snarling—waving their hands like pawn-shop owners haggling over a counter. But they jumped from their boxes and scattered when they saw High Pockets Hague.

"What's your hurry?" jeered Washout. "Stick around an' see the excitement."

But the orators didn't care for that brand. They knew when to quit, and that time, they could see, had come round.

Hague dismounted before the Copper Bar, tossed his reins across the rack. One after the other he pulled the two pistols from the waistband of his Levis, examined their mechanism carefully and thrust them back out of sight.

"Just stay where you are," he told Washout.

Then he was pushing through the doors into a dimmer light than that provided by the noon-time sun. He got his back instantly against a wall and kept it there till his eyes absorbed this change. There were not many men in the place. Those that he saw looked startled; looked regretful that they were not elsewhere.

High Pockets slouched against the wall and looked them over, one by one. "You still hangin' around, Caprosa? Surprised you didn't take that warnin' I posted for Organ's friends."

Caprosa's swarthy cheeks were like a mask hacked out of bullet lead; his eyes were frightened, bulging.

"Better get out now," drawled High Pockets coldly, "before I change my mind. Don't let me see you round after dark."

His glance passed on, jerking up at a man sitting stiff at a table. "You here, too, Taiban?" The remark sounded mildly astonished. He fished the makings from a pocket and left-handedly curled a smoke, the while he looked at the man consideringly. His head tipped then to send a cold-eyed glance through the wooden-faced crew at the bar. Looking back at Taiban, he scratched a match along the wall, touched the flame to his cigarette. "Your brother showed yet?"

Tight-lipped, Taiban shook his head. He watched Hague with a gleaming care.

"You better be driftin', too," Hague said, and of the barman asked; "Frodsham round?"

"Back room," the bartender muttered. He jerked his head toward the door.

Hague's glance flicked again to Caprosa and

Taiban. "Last warnin', boys. Don't let sundown catch you in these parts."

Caprosa crawled from his chair like an oft-beaten cur and slunk out of the house without argument. But Taiban's copper face bloated poisonously. "You goddamn fool!" he swore. "Better get out yourself while you're able! Just wait'll Clay Frodsham finds you're back!"

High Pockets laughed. Shoving open the door he strode into Frodsham's office.

But the gambler wasn't there. There wasn't anybody there. Wheeling round he came on out and, approaching the bar, told the man behind it: "I guess you were mistaken, friend. The chickens have all climbed off the roost."

In the back-bar mirror his arrested glance caught a tag-end of movement started by Taiban's diving reach.

A gun crashed thunderously. Flame and smoke belched wickedly from a hand beside Hague's half-turned body.

Taiban, up out of his chair, hung crouched like a thing on strings. Then his lean-whipped body buckled, dropping him forward across a table that flattened beneath his weight.

No person in that long room moved.

With each man frozen solid, the slatted bat-wings suddenly bulged. Frodsham's hoarse voice shouted; "What the bloody hell's—" That far he got and stopped, his wide eyes bright on High Pocket's features.

"I'm practicin' my draw," Hague said. "You wantin' a demonstration?"

Frodsham's hooded glance passed from

Hague's cool face to the still smoking gun in his hand. A kind of pallor wheeled across his cheeks.

He yanked his glance away, slamming it across the place in a raking half-circle that jerked up sharp, afraid, astounded, when it reached the dead man sprawled across the table.

"Ain't you wantin' a demonstration?" High Pockets urged.

Shock edged the tautened lines of Frodsham's cheeks. The cheeks themselves had taken on an unpleasant, mottled appearance; and his deepened breathing rasped repeated scratches across the room's scared quiet.

He seemed to shiver as he met the outlander's mocking stare. "No." His voice sounded husky. "No—I reckon not."

"I'm some surprised," High Pockets told him, grinning. "I kinda gathered from some things that fella said, that you'd be shootin' me on sight. I understand you're sheriff now. Ain't that a part of your duties?—like foreclosin' on the widders an' orphans an' gangin' up on defenseless girls?"

A saturnine humor showed through Hague's cold gaze; it started sweat on Frodsham's face.

With tremendous effort the tinhorn sheriff got a hold on himself. He passed a slow hand across his forehead, stared a moment, fascinated by the film of moisture the hand displayed.

But Hague had become impatient of this farce. He said very definitely: "This is your last warning, Frodsham. Keep out of Rafter business. Leave Rafter's things alone."

With a quick hard look he wheeled away, went pushing through the doors.

* * *

"Where now?" asked Washout, grinning.

"I'd like to get a line on Ballard. But I reckon we better hunt Wesley. Whereabouts does he have his office?"

"Just up the street a bit. See that red pine buildin'?"

Hague climbed into his saddle.

In front of Wallabye's office Washout grunted: "Nobody home." There was a padlock on the door. A placard tacked to the wall at one side announced the place as headquarters for Amalgamated Copper.

Hague dismounted and, with a pocket knife, carefully removed the tacks. Turning the placard blank side outward he nailed it up again. With a stub of pencil he printed in large black characters:

**FRAUDULENT
STOCK PROMOTERS
WHO VALUE THEIR HEALTH
WILL TAKE
THE FIRST STAGE OUT.**

H.P. Hague.

25

DREAD REALIZATION

Having dispatched Washout to collect his squatter friends, locate Jim Thompson if he could and Monkey Janes, and meet him with these men in front of Wallabye's place tonight at twelve, High Pockets rode out into the chaparral, hobbled his bronc and curled up under a juniper.

It was dark when he awakened. Stars shone down like sleepy mockers and all the range loomed bluely argent under a yellow moon. A breeze made gentle whisperings among scrub oaks' dusty foliage, and as he strapped the gear upon his roan he thought a little sadly, of the things that might have been.

But there was no kind of use thinking such thoughts. Nostalgia and repining were for those who could afford it; Hague could not. He was not underestimating Frodsham. He might bluff and bully, but he was a wolf; you could warn and threaten till hell froze, but Frodsham would never quit. Hague knew to the fraction how far the gambler's guts would take him; knew too well how the towering ambition and lust for vengeance that were conflicting forces in the gambler's makeup would drive the man far past the point where shattered nerves would crack. Frodsham was out to control this country utterly; only Rafter stood in his way and nothing but death would stop him. He might be scared, he might go in trembling fear of retribution, but the grasping ambition that ruled his life would drive him to attainment of whatever fantastic goal he'd set his heart on.

He must be killed like any other romping beast who threatened men's lives and happiness. And Wallabye Wesley, Ballard, Branton and Caprosa must be driven from the country; or, if they stood at bay like cornered rats and fought—eliminated. No other way could Rosalee and Rafter ever know any peace.

What he had to do, Hague would do—regardless of the consequences.

Thoughts of Rosalee came and smoothed the scowl from his bronzed features. He did not blame her for treating him as she had; she had named him right—a roughneck gun fighter with no good in him but the speed to trip a trigger. If there'd been anything better in him it was gone—wiped out by three years of turbulence. For a time he'd dared presume to dream, and there was no denying that the dream had held a precious fascination for one whose waking hours had been filled as Hague's had; but that was past, the dream was gone, he was facing bleak reality.

He knew now and could safely admit—to himself—that he had fallen in love with the girl. But that must be the end of it. He would do what little he could for her, then ride on over the hump.

No man in his position could admit his sentiment publicly. He could not go to her and declare it; he had not the right. He'd left too many enemies scattered through this Southwest country. His luck wouldn't last forever. Some day a rifle would bark from the brush or rimrock. That would be all, he knew.

He stood in his stirrups and peered around. The lights of Bonanza winked up from the hollow. Impatience tugged at his shoulders; impatience to get this chore done and be gone.

But he'd time to spend before Washout got back with the squatters. Might be a good idea to look over Branton's Lucky Bug; he was curious about that ore. It might be ore from the missing wagons . . .

He knew where the Lucky Bug lay—he had learned its location from Washout. Lifting his reins, he sank back in the saddle. He sent the roan down at a walk.

Washout had said there were Mexicans always on guard at the Lucky Bug's mouth, but High Pockets did not see any. He knew Branton for a tricky customer, though, and thought it highly possible the man had laid some kind of trap. He crouched down in the brush, deciding to watch for a while and consider. The roan he'd left tied in some alders 'way back, making chance of discovery remote as he could.

He crouched there, hunkered on his bootheels, for a good bit over an hour. But there was no sign of Branton's *pelados*. Either the men had gone off to town or they were in the tunnel someplace.

Hague was tired of waiting. Squatting round

194

this way gave a man too much time for reflection, and High Pockets had burned his bridges. He wanted no regrets.

He wriggled cautiously forward; crawled closer. Rising in the shadow of some mesquite, he peered into the black opacity of the tunnel. There was nothing to be seen; no sound was to be heard. Stepping carefully, he ventured in.

The place was foul with the smell of oil, burnt powder fumes and sweat. His steps echoed curiously in that timbered passage. There was an air-pipe along the roof that led off to unguessed depths. Hague tapped it with his six-gun, but no reply came back. It looked like he was alone.

He moved more boldly now. He struck a match and scouted till he found a stub of candle in a tin can. This he lighted and, with its reflected rays driving back the gloom, proceeded rapidly till he came to where Jake Branton had sunk his shaft.

It was a good-sized hole, but showed no great expenditure of money. It was not timbered. A wooden ladder, rigged to the wall with two-by-fours, led downward out of sight.

With his rude light held in left hand Hague got onto the ladder and started down the shaft. He went ten feet before he struck the ore. Balancing his tincan lamp precariously on a rung, he cautiously got out his skinning knife and, tight-lipped, got to work. Five minutes later a large chunk of ore let go its hold of the sidewall and went hurtling into the murk. The sound of a splash came up from below as Hague nodded grimly. Washout and Charlie were right—this Lucky Bug Lode was salted. The only ore here had come from the Rafter wagons!

Hague tensed suddenly, listening.

Were those voices he had heard?

He doused the light and held his breath . . .

Yes—they came more plainly now. Two men talking. Up above, someplace. Branton and another man—it sounded to Hague like Ballard.

Then Branton laughed. "I guess this'll hold the bastard!" Then the sound of muffled bootsteps thumping out a hurried retreat.

Hague clung to the ladder, wondering. Had Branton meant *him?* Had those birds known he was down here?

He clung there, listening in the darkness, a curious odor tugging at his consciousness. Damn funny, he thought uneasily; kind of smelled like powder—

Realization struck him suddenly like a knife between the shoulders. That hissing sound, as though of steam escaping—that smell! Good God! *They'd lit a fuse!*

26

PAYOFF

Frantically, made desperate by knowledge of the fate these men had planned for him, Hague started up the ladder. Hand over reaching hand he went, mounting steadily higher while, somewhere in this unplumbed dark, the burning fuse crept ever nearer the high explosive it must lead to.

He could not see the hand before him; could only guess where each next rung was and grab for it, and hope. He had not ever known what fright could do to a man, till now. He had seen men sweat in its grip, of course, but had never guessed they could feel so cold. . . . His teeth began to chatter.

God! Would he never reach the ladder's top?

And then he *had* reached it, and was tumbling, sprawling in a nightmare fall—not far, not half his height, and the ground was solid, damp, a-drip. He got clawed hands into its slimy surface, stumbled to his feet; stared round him wildly.

The powder smell was stronger . . . .

Was that the tunnel's mouth?—*that patch?*—
that dim, vague loom of lesser murk among the
swirling blackness?

The hiss had grown much louder now; a
spluttering, rushing roar of sound that filled the
tumultuous dark—dire warning of disaster.

And then he saw it—the burning fuse! It was
between him and the tunnel's mouth; dull,
glowing, like a fog-screened sparkler.

How long—? He could never reach the tunnel's
mouth in time! He knew in his bones he couldn't
make it; couldn't get outside before that hissing
thing made contact.

Could he break it off? Could he stamp it out?
Could he get there quick enough to stop it?

He tried—he ran with all the strength of strong
hard muscles, but knew before he reached it that
he was late.

Too late.

He'd neither time nor room. The glowing of
those shooting sparks disclosed it. Not half an
inch of fuse was left between that burning end
and neat stacked sticks of dynamite.

With one swift bound, crouched low, he scooped
sticks, fuse and all aloft and hurled them toward
the tunnel's mouth.

There was a blinding flash—

Even when Hague met Washout and the others
in front of Wallabye's office at twelve his ears
still rang, and every little while, his knees shook
from reaction. Even then he had to keep feeling of
himself, it seemed so damned incredible he could
really have escaped. But Washout had news that

drove all thought of that near disaster from his mind.

"We're sunk!" he snared at High Pockets. "Sold out an' down the river! Wallabye's pulled it off, the slick talkin', thievin' snipe!"

Janes said: "He's into Rafter for half the mine—"

Washout blared: "Half hell! The weasel's talked her outa fifty-one percent an' put the pressure on already! Called a meetin' of the stockholders—which is him an' her—this mornin' an' declared he's obliged to levy an assessment. On account of a piled-up deficit or some damn thing in the mine's past operations! I say God damn his soul to hell! Buy God, he oughta be boiled in lard!"

Hague stared. "You're—you're sure of this?"

"Hell, yes!" swore Lunkan bitterly, and all the squatters nodded.

"He's given her till tonight t' pay," said Kettle-Belly grimly. "They're out there now, I reckon, the whole damn crowd—like a bunch of stinkin' buzzards."

"Who is?" Hague demanded staring. "Kinda late for callers, ain't it?"

Washout muttered. "That's the time he give 'er—till twelve tonight to get the money or—Hell! he set it late so's the whole devil's spawn of 'em could git there! Who? Why Ballard, Frodsham, himself an' Branton! Prob'ly have three-four of his gunnies along, too, jest in case Roberts gets the wind up. Them Rafter boys is pretty mad, but—Hell! what do they amount to? Cow-stealers showed them boys up—"

Hague broke in, saying puzzledly: "I still don't see but what she'll come out of this all right. You talk like Rafter's whipped already—or damn quick goin' to be. How much is this assessment fixed for?"

"Ten thousand dollars!" Thompson muttered. "Ten thousand bucks apiece—*on the first goddamn assessment!*"

"The whole thing stinks," snarled Kettle-Belly.

Washout asked: "Member Frodsham sayin' how he'd smash the Rafter? Well, this is it. Roberts says they they lost four hundred head of cattle—"

"But they lost them legal," Thompson pointed out. "Just like this minin' deal—so goddamn legal you can taste it! That Kendall crook's the slickest blackleg in the state. The four hundred steers," he said to High Pockets, "was impounded. Hoof an' mouth disease, the inspector claimed—an' started them for the border!"

"At least," Hague said, "Rafter can stand this assessment stung. There's a deal more money than—"

"Not no more, there ain't," snapped Washout, cursing. "Some skunk talked Rosalee into switchin' her account to the Bonanza Trust an' the damn crib's just been gutted! Hear that shoutin'? Crowd's just found out. Three-four floursacks cleaned it durin' supper—ain't enough dinero left in the vault t' buy a kid a rattle!"

Hague got it then, and his cheeks went white as wood-ash. The sharpness of his glance was an arresting thing. His voice rapped at them taciturnly. "What's Wallabye doin' if she can't meet this assessment?"

"Puttin' her out, bag an' baggage—tonight," Thompson muttered sullenly.

Hague said: "What the hell we waitin' for?" and several tin-shack nesters cheered. But Janes growled: "Too late now," and several others nodded. "The deal's all signed. Wallabye's got fifty-one percent; he's within his rights. An' the law will—"

A thin cold smile curled Hague's lips bleakly. "This here's all the law I'm needin'." He tapped the handles of his guns and the group fell quiet.

A new voice broke the deadlock. A stranger with a horse in tow said gently: "Mind if I go along? I'm middlin' fair with a shotgun."

Before Hague could speak Janes snapped: "It ain't no use. Frodsham's sheriff, an' he swings a lot of influence; he's a particular friend of this slick Wesley's. We've lost our chance. It's too damn late—"

"It may," Hague said with his lips curled back, "be too damn late to save that girl her mine. But we'll be in plenty of time, Mister Janes, to empty three-four hats." Abruptly then, that wild fury he'd been holding in check so long broke bounds, broke through his guard and gave a new and wicked slanting to his cheeks. "Were you born yellow natural, Janes? Or is it just the way these store lights show you up?"

Hague sat tipped forward in his saddle, a biting scorn in the raking glance he put across them. There was violence vibrant in every sinew of his drawn-taut figure. "God damn you!" he cried in a headlong rush of passion. "Stay safe in town like the pack of slinkin' coyotes that you are. I can do this job alone, by God!"

* * *

It was a quarter to one, with the gaunt outlines of Rafter's buildings looming black against the stars, when Hague came in sight of the ranch headquarters. The squatters were strung out behind him and he waited grimly till they all came up. He said: "We'll leave the horses here. Our crowd's inside the ranch house—there's their horses racked beside the porch. Spread out an' get around it. Keep your eyes on the ranch house windows an' don't fire till you get my orders. Remember—there's a girl inside it; we don't want to see her hit. All ready?"

The lanky stranger packing the shotgun touched him on the arm. "You goin' to warn 'em?"

"Yes, I'll warn them once. After that it's up to them. Ready, boys? Let's go."

Hague waited till he saw the men spread out and vanish among the shadows. He strode erectly forward, big fists hanging at his sides. Ten feet from the porch he stopped. With lifted voice he slammed his challenge at the house. His only answer was a dousing of the lights.

His voice rose dryly: "Might's well come out now, boys. We're not leavin' here till you do."

"What the hell you want?" It was Ballard's voice asking that question.

"We want to see you gents off of Rafter," Hague said quietly, and somebody laughed.

A long stillness settled then, broke suddenly by the sharp flat crack of a rifle from the rear. Some fool had fired regardless of orders and the fat was in the fire. He knew it by the choked-off scream that instantly followed. They'd fight now; nothing could stop it.

A high-pitched yell of rage burst raggedly from the shadows. Windows blossomed with orange flame. Above and through the babel of shouts roared the wicked crash of gunfire, pagan anthem to a song of death.

Guns poured out their mad staccato, streams of lead beat the earthen walls like Yaqui drums heard from the distance. Hague dropped to a knee, coolly waiting for a target. The thud of gun-crash rocked the air. Lead sliced past him; kicked dust spurts from the ground around. A close bullet brushed his hat, its sound rushing from the left where he'd no good reason for expecting danger. He whirled his body half around, a soft oath dropping from tight lips as he keened the black, banked shadows beneath the trees. A man was out there somewhere, one of that group who'd come here with him. Tipping backward suddenly he sprawled on his shoulders, seeing muzzle-light bloom from a thicket where no tin-shack nester had a right to be. He came up to his feet, hurling his body three paces sideward, a gun-butt thumping his right hand heavily as he caught brief sight of a slinking shape among the brush-thrown shadows.

He fired again and saw the shape topple toward him, fall grotesquely and roll from the thicket to disclose the moonglow the twisted face of Monkey Bill Janes.

A quick sharp sound broke back of him, spinning him round to face the house as three men broke from the door, spilled out with blazing weapons across the darkened porch.

He saw the dim pale gleam of faces, then they were breaking from the roof gloom, rushing toward him; cursing, firing, crouched low down with faces bitter. Ballard, Branton and a man he did not know. With lead spatting all around him he held his fire, calling on them to stop.

But they came on. Ballard's burly form showed through the swirling half light—Branton's tigerish smirk.

Hague had no choice. Smashing lead hammered Ballard against the porch, pinned him swaying with bulging eyes and both hands squeezed against his chest. Flame-jet stabbed from Hague's left hip. Lead was tugging at his neckerchief, at his vest; spashing dust across his boots. Branton was frantic; fright still bugged his stare when High Pockets dropped him.

Hague whirled round. But the other man was gone.

The guns had stilled. With the snarl of rage-hoarsened voices in his ears, Hague crossed the porch, hurried into the house. A lamp had been lit in the living room, its light picking out savage faces glowering across leveled rifles poked menacingly through the windows. The squatters were in change.

Hague saw the girl standing white beside the table. There was a tough-faced man lying dead by the back door, and the wide-open barrier showed Kettle-Belly and Washout lounging just outside with grins above their leveled pistols. Disheveled, Clay Roberts stood by the fireplace talking in lowered tones to the shotgun-packing stranger.

Wallabye, gray-cheeked, shaking, stood near

Rosalee; and Frodsham in a bloody shirt sat scowling, silent, in a rocker beside the stove, ignoring the things around him, staring fixedly at Hague.

"You better let me go," snarled Wallabye loudly. "You ain't got nothing on me. I didn't have a thing to do with this—matter of fact, I did my best to keep the gunplay out of it—as Miss Rosalee will tell you!" He looked at the girl; Hague looked, too. She nodded wearily.

"What about your mine," Hague said. "Taken it away from you, ain't he?"

She shrugged, not meeting his eyes.

"What I've had to do," muttered Wallabye thickly, "was perfectly legal. I wouldn't have done it for the world except—except I had to defend myself. A man's first duty," he said with an attempt at dignity, "is to protect his business investments. Miss Parshall couldn't find the money to meet an assessment the company was forced to—"

"That's enough," Hague said. "I know all about it. Same kind of deal you pulled on that widow at Globe; same way you got hold of the Copperstain over in Nevada last year. I believe you'd eat out of the same plate with a snake—if you could get up high enough to stick your face in."

Wallabye glowered at him, furious. But he kept his tongue in his mouth, and kept the mouth tightly closed.

"I recall you asked me once if I remembered you," Hague said. "Well the answer's yes. I remember you for the crookedest promoter north of Death Valley. You're the skunk that gutted

Redona an' left it flat in the middle of the night. I'd not be surprised at all to learn you're the man that cleaned out the Bonanza Trust—"

"That's a goddamn lie!" shrieked Wesley, shaking. "I never went near the place tonight! It was Ballard, Branton an'—" He stopped, white-cheeked, eyes startled, realizing suddenly what he'd done; looking slanchways at the drained, inscrutable face of Clayton Frodsham.

But Frodsham didn't look at him. He made no comment at all. He sat there huddled in the rocker, chin on chest, with his eyes glaring wickedly at Hague.

Roberts growled with a voice high-pitched and nervous: "You might's well tell the rest of it now. By God, if you don't, we'll see how you look in tar and feathers!"

Wesley licked his lips uneasily. He'd inadvertently betrayed a dangerous knowledge. He stood uncertain now whether to go on or try to recant.

Hague said: "I guess we can figure the rest of it. You an' Frodsham made a deal—"

"I didn't have nothing to do with it!" Wallabye snapped. "I'll be damned if I'll be dragged into it. I overheard Ballard an' Branton talkin' on the way out here this evenin'. They'd fixed up the deal with Frodsham without my knowledge!" He glared at Frodsham's silent figure. "My own partner, by God! Out to do me like I was some Eastern sucker! I can't believe it hardly yet—"

"You willin' to go your oath on this?" Hague asked, and Wallabye scowled. "No," he said, uprightly. "What Mr. Frodsham may have done has nothing to do with *my* actions. I don't act the sneak with any man. What he's done's between himself and God."

"Yes—very noble," Hague murmured dryly. He started across the door, intending to ask Washout something. He had his back squarely turned on Frodsham when—

"*Look out!*" screamed Rosalee, frightened.

Hague threw himself to the left and spun, his wide lips parted, aslant with malice.

Too late Frodsham realized his error. He saw the gun streaking up in Hague's right hand; fired hurriedly, frantically—terrified.

But Hague stood grinning wickedly. He fired just once.

Frodsham, out of his chair, half-crouched, leaned suddenly forward as though to meet that leaping flame. For a second he seemed to hang there, poised in an awkward bow. The hinges of his knees collapsed abruptly, spilling him, crumpled, on the floor.

"*Geez!*" cried Washout, startled. And Kettle-Belly said: "Some shootin'!"

"Self-defense," remarked the stranger with the shotgun, and tapped a hand against Wallabye's chest. "You'll have to come with me, my friend. I have a warrant for you— Just save your breath. It's a penitentiary offence to use the mails the way you been doing." He smiled remotely at the expression on Wallabye's countenance. "You're under arrest, Mr. Wesley, an' I'd advise you not to make me any trouble."

He thrust a hand in Wallabye's coat, bringing forth a folded, crinkly paper that was black with fine spaced print. Still smiling faintly he passed the document to Rosalee. "My advice to you, Miss Parshall, would be to tear that business up. A criminal's got no right to be making contracts anyway." Then, suddenly sobering, "Come along, my fine-feathered friend," he said to Wallabye. "It's time for stock promoters to close up shop."

"Well," remarked High Pockets, after all the others had gone, "I expect I'd better be on my way, ma'am. Got a sight of travelin' to do between now an' dawn."

"You—you're not thinking of leaving this Black Range country?"

Hague looked down at his hat; stood awhile as though considering. "Well, yes, ma'am," he said at last. He looked at her tiredly. His voice was devoid of hope. "There's nothing for me here—"

"Why, Pete! There's me—"

Rosalee seemed unconscious of the mangling of her grammer. But Hague wasn't noticing, either. He was staring at her, startled. He said: "Rosalee—! Do you mean that?"

"Of course," she cried, and, blushing, crept into his arms.

He stood there, stiffly, paralyzed; a film of sweat across his face. "You—you—Surely you can't mean this, ma'am? After—"

"I've seen what a little fool I've been—this business of Wallabye showed me. I'll be different from now on, Pete—honest. I've seen the truth at last."

"But—but you couldn't love a man like me—"

"I've loved you all the time," she said, and High Pockets said no more.